SACRÉ CŒUR

E COMMERCE

OPÉRA

MADELEINE

LES GRANDS
BOULEVARDS

LE LUXE

CORDE

PLACE
VENDOME

L'ARTISANAT

LOUVRE

SEINE

HOTEL DE VILLE

Paris

Wish you were here!

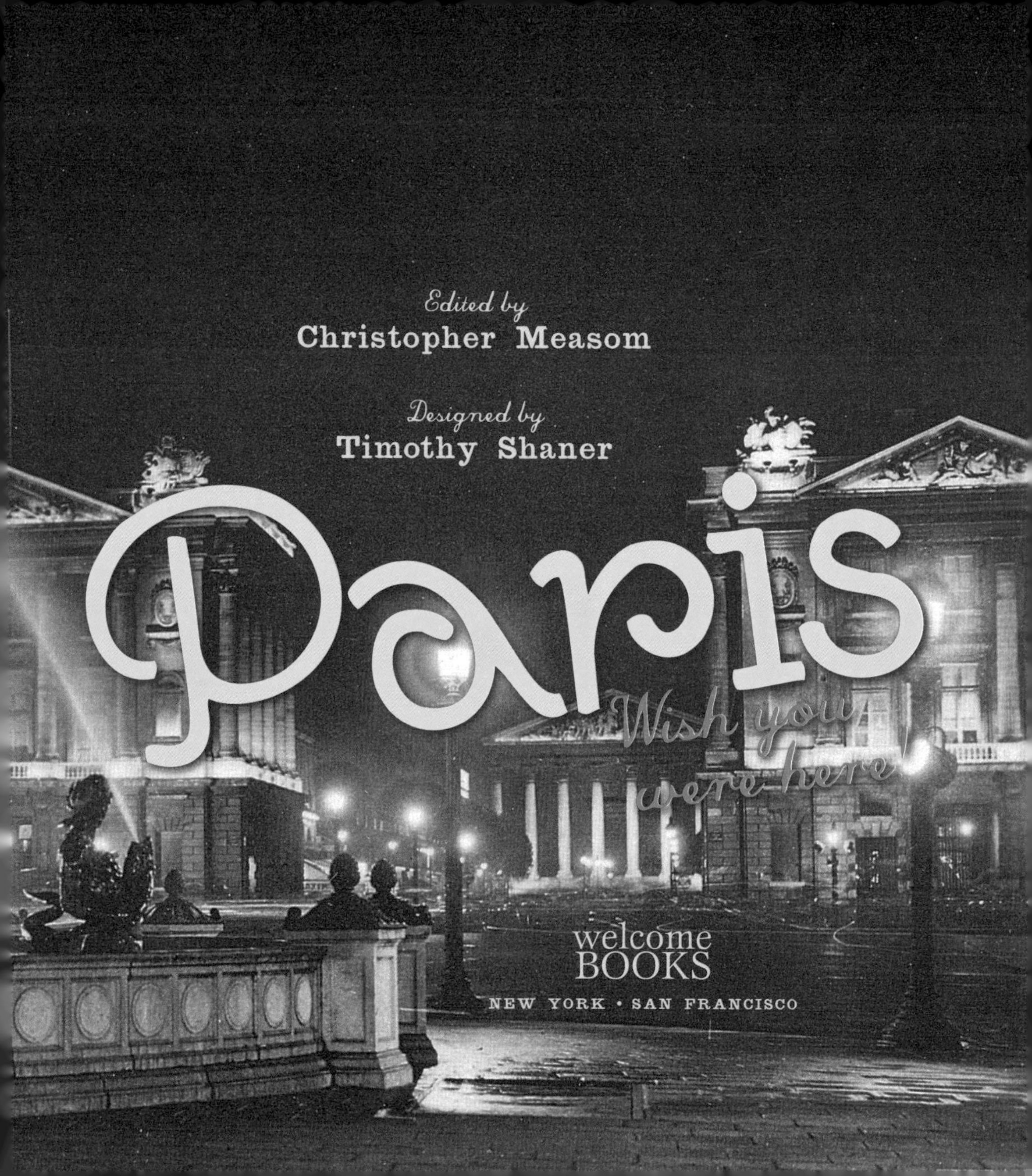

Edited by
Christopher Measom

Designed by
Timothy Shaner

Paris

*Wish you
were here!*

welcome
BOOKS

NEW YORK · SAN FRANCISCO

Published in 2008 by Welcome Books®
An imprint of Welcome Enterprises, Inc.
6 West 18th Street, New York, NY 10011
Tel: 212-989-3200; Fax: 212-989-3205
www.welcomebooks.com

Publisher: Lena Tabori
Project Director: Natasha Tabori Fried   Project Assistant: Kara Mason

Copyright © 2008 Night & Day Design LLC.
www.nightanddaydesign.biz
Additional copyright information on page 272.

Library of Congress Cataloging-in-Publication Data

Paris : wish you were here / edited by Christopher Measom ;
designed by Timothy Shaner.
    p. cm.
 ISBN 978-1-59962-043-5
 1. Paris (France)--Description and travel. I. Measom, Christopher.
    DC707.P257 2008
    914.4'3610484--dc22   2007042779

Printed in Singapore

FIRST EDITION

1 3 5 7 9 10 8 6 4 2

Contents

Contents

Les Chansons

LE QUARTIER LATIN S'EST, LUI AUSSI, MODERNISÉ :
LES ÉLÉGANTS COMPTOIRS À DÉBIT RAPIDE-Y
REMPLACENT LES BRASSERIES DE JADIS

Contents

Foreword

by Christopher Measom

During my junior year abroad in Spain it was so hot and so dry that by November, we only had running water a few hours a day. This prompted me, and some fellow suffering students, to seek relief by going as far north as we could over a long holiday weekend. Paris, a 24-hour train ride away, was the destination we picked (a first for all of us), and when we arrived it was overcast, cool, and heavenly (there was running water all day long, too). As we left Austerlitz station in search of our hotel, beauty and elegance were my first impressions. The architecture was gorgeous, the people were chic, and *excusez-mois* replaced the sharp elbows of the widows on the bus back in Sevilla. Although I adore Spain, Paris instantly found a place in my heart.

Low on funds, we bunked three to a room on that trip (the one I was in had stripped wallpaper covering every surface except the floor), and eating at a restaurant was out of the question. But I didn't care. Just wandering from shop to shop—the *boulangerie* for bread, the *fromagerie* for cheese, the *patisserie* for dessert—with the Eiffel Tower in the background was more than enough for me. A bottle of wine, a mini quiche, and *frites* from the vendor at the corner rounded out the typical meal we ate picnic-style back in the room. I have no memory of going to the Louvre or to any museums even though I was minoring in art history . . . but I must have. The things I remember most are buying my French-English dictionary at dusty, book-filled Shakespeare & Company and learning the word *tranche* (slice) while ordering *pâté de foie gras de canard* (duck liver pâté)—something I had never heard of before but will never forget.

The next time I saw Paris I stayed for two months. I had graduated from college and had been working about two years (the career-less kind of paying-the-rent drudgery) when I thought, *Let me try living in Paris for a while*. So I enrolled at the Alliance Française on

Foreword

the Boulevard Raspail and quickly fell in with an international group (an experience very similar to David Sedaris's piece on page 195, except my teacher was fun and gave us tips on how to eat cheaply and take full advantage of all the city had to offer). Spanish, Swiss, Irish, Brazilian, and Indonesian, our motley crew struggled with and reveled in Parisian life. For the first month I shared a room in a pension with Remigio, who worked for the Italian railroad and was trying to improve his French. It was cheap, included breakfast, was within five minutes of class, and was directly across from the Jardin du Luxembourg. The only odd thing was that the two Eastern European guys living in the next room—who never spoke—had to pass through our room to get to theirs. The pension was booked the second month so I moved on to a very tiny room on the very top floor of a very cheap (and cold) hotel. If I wanted a shower it was 10 francs extra (somewhere around $1.50 back then), but the sort-of-cock eyed cleaning girl took a liking to me and would slip me the key whenever she could. At that time I was reading Hemingway's *A Moveable Feast* (page 91) and totally related to his visions of eating the pigeons from the park. Nonetheless, I took my teacher's frequent encouragement, *profitez,* seriously and went to every exhibit, every performance, every lecture, and every movie that my student card would get me into. And, *comme ça,* I really got to know Paris.

One night, walking home from a long, late dinner of wine and intense discussions of art and politics, as I crossed the bridge from the Île de la Cité into the medieval area of the fifth arrondissement just past Notre Dame, I thought, *This city couldn't be better.* And then it began to snow and I fell deeper in love with Paris.

The French I picked up on that trip helped me get a job as assistant to Pierre Moulin (the founder of the French fabric store Pierre Deux) when I returned to New York. Although I loved learning about *l'Art de Vivre* of France and using my French in that job, by far the best fringe benefit was that Pierre had an apartment near the Eiffel Tower that he let me use from time to time. On one trip he arranged for my first meal at a real

Parisian restaurant, le Boeuf sur le Toit. I used my best French to decipher the menu and ordered *langoustine* hoping a lobster would arrive on my plate. When the waiter left, the man at the next table leaned over and said, "You ordered everything you wanted."

This past summer I rented an old and charming apartment in the Marais from Alexis, an opera singer with the dramatic beauty of Elizabeth Taylor circa 1970. There I ate cold cereal with bits of dark chocolate in it for breakfast, discovered that laundry never really dries in France, and learned how to say "There is no Internet service" while arguing with the cable guys. Naturally I also had lots of visitors. When Tim and Emily came we got a lecture on cheese at the rue Montorgueil market, heard the organ play in the ancient Saint-Eustache cathedral, and drank champagne while making fun of the wacky Japanese opera we saw (well, they saw it; I mostly napped on the velvet couch in our box). Next Alannah and Finn (who are 10 and 7) came and we looked (in vain) for a plot of grass on which to play badminton. Bottom line: You risk arrest (as one kind woman warned us) by playing on the grass in almost any Parisian park. Still, we managed to find a spot in front of a magnificent limestone palace. Then we sailed boats in the Jardin du Luxembourg, looked at the hairy asses (a native donkey) at the menagerie in the Jardin des Plantes, and sipped sweet tea at the pink marble Grande Mosquée de Paris (the great mosque of Paris).

Writing about travel over the last decade has given me the opportunity to see lots of the world, and yet I still daydream about Paris. I'm drawn by the aesthetics: the stunning views and monuments, the abundant art and fashion, the fabulous food. I also love the people. Yes, they can be somewhat aloof to strangers (as you might be if your town had been invaded so many times), but they also connect. There is always a "Bonjour, monsieur" upon entering a shop and an "Au revoir" or "Bonne journée" when leaving. I love that.

Now I'm thinking about my next trip. Lunch among the bling at the Baccarat Museum, maybe a cooking class at the Cordon Bleu (like Julia Child) . . . and always a café crème, *pain au chocolat,* and people-watching at my favorite café. ■

To know Paris is to know a great deal.

—Henry Miller

ARRONDISSEMENT 1ER

This is the geographic center of Paris—the place kings called home, the location of the most famous museum on earth (the Louvre), the most famous gardens (the Tuileries) and a shopaholic's dream come true. To the east le Forum des Halles, formerly "the belly of Paris" (which was the primary food market for centuries), is now a shopping mall surrounded by pedestrian streets filled with bargain shops. The arcaded rue de Rivoli, the spine of the arrondissement, offers antiques and souvenirs. And toward the western end of the neighborhood is the stunning 18th-century architectural masterpiece Place Vendôme. Perfume boutiques and jewelry stores like Cartier and Boucheron encircle a 44-meter-high column with Napoleon (dressed as Caesar) on top. At number 15 Mr. Ritz opened his hotel—the epitome of luxury and elegance—in 1898. Coco Chanel lived here for over 30 years and the bar, having been a favorite of Hemingway (and F. Scott Fitzgerald), is now called Bar Hemingway.

Amid all the buzzing activity there are pockets of calm. The often overlooked Palais Royale gardens lie just a stone's throw from the Louvre, while two gems—the Musée de l'Orangerie and the Jeu de Paume (antidotes to the gargantuan Louvre and its never-ending crowds)—lie just across the Tuileries.

Most quiet of all, however, is the Place Dauphine, a charming square hidden behind the Palais de Justice at the very tip of Île de la Cité. Sit with a book here or watch a cutthroat pétanque match.

ar·ron·disse·ment *n* (f) (1807) an administrative district of some large French cities. Traditionally written in Roman numerals (5th = Ve), now more commonly 5è or 5ème (cinquième).

PARIS
Une Petite Histoire

lthough there is evidence of a settlement in the Bercy area of Paris about 6,000 years ago, there is much more known about the Celtic Parisii tribe who showed up 3,000 or 4,000 years later, around 250 BC, to do some fishing along the Seine. It seems they lived peacefully in a small community on the Île de la Cité for about 300 years until the Romans arrived, took over, and changed the name to Lutetia (Lutèce in French). Around 212 the name was changed to Paris (after the local tribe), and 200 years of civil unrest followed as barbarians menaced the village.

Things came to a head in 451 when Attila the Hun nearly invaded. But the city was saved—so it is said—by Sainte Geneviève's prayers, which are credited with turning the Hun south to invade elsewhere. Unfortunately, 13 years later her prayers were not answered, as Childeric (the Frank) did invade.

Things went well with the Franks (Clovis I brought Christianity) for about 300 years until the Vikings took their turn pillaging in the 9th century.

From the 12th to the 13th centuries Paris began—in a very basic way—to take its modern shape. Notre Dame Cathedral was built

(establishing a center of religious and government life), the Sorbonne was founded (consolidating the Left Bank as a center of international study and learning), and some businessmen got together and established a merchant's group headquartered on the Right Bank (a precursor to today's center of finance). During those years the Palais du Louvre was also begun, as was the food market Les Halles, and Louis IX (later Saint Louis) built Sainte Chapelle to house Jesus' crown of thorns, which he bought from Baldwin II in 1239.

The rest of the 13th century went downhill fast. The Hundred Years' War between England and France over succession to the throne was followed by the arrival of one of the most deadly pandemics in the

Above: Queen Isabeau of Bavaria at the gates of Paris, 1389.

history of humankind—the Black Plague. Plague continued to vex the city during the 14th century, which led to political unrest and popular uprisings. As a result the monarchy built the infamous Bastille prison. By 1453, when the war ended, the city was in ruins.

It wasn't until the 16th century, when the monarchy caught wind of the Italian Renaissance, that things began to improve. They got even better through the 17th century, known as le Grand Siècle (the grand century), as Louis XIV (the Sun King) instituted his plan to make Paris a "New Rome" (although he moved the court to Versailles). The Age of Reason followed: art, science, and philosophy flourished; and Paris suddenly found itself the intellectual and cultural capital of the world.

Toward the end of the 18th century, however, the Seven Years' War,

debt stemming from contributions made to America's War for Independence, and a very bad harvest in 1788 left the coffers empty. All the glory ended in tears (and quite a bit of blood) when an angry mob stormed the Bastille on July 14, 1789. The revolution had begun. The downfall of the monarchy was imminent and a

Above: Storming the Bastille. Previous pages: The Consecration of Emperor Napoleon I and Coronation of Empress Josephine *by Jacques Louis David.*

violent turmoil that would have repercussions for the next 100 years followed.

The city was rescued (sort of) by Napoleon, a general during the revolution, whose (very successful) methods of crowd control included firing cannons point-blank into the mob. He famously crowned himself emperor during a glorious ceremony in Notre Dame Cathedral in 1804. Under him France became a strong military power, but his reign came to an end in 1815 after the battle at Waterloo.

During the 19th century the monarchy came again and went again, a new Napoleon (Louis-Napoleon Bonaparte, or Napoleon III, the nephew of the first Napoleon) also came and went, and Paris pretty much became the city you see today—especially after 1850, when Baron Haussmann was commissioned to transform it from a pestilent warren of medieval streets into a monumental city of wide avenues and open spaces.

The arrondissements were reorganized and fixed as they are today; slums were cleared; sewers were greatly improved; railroads, grand buildings, and monuments were built; and public parks were added to the city.

Unfortunately, Napoleon III took on the Prussians—to disastrous effect. The city, under siege from September 1870 to January 1871, nearly starved to death. All the animals in the zoo—except the monkeys— were eaten, and, toward the end, cat, dog, and even rat regularly

appeared on Parisian menus. The government collapsed, and the Commune of Paris took over for two extraordinarily bloody months.

That same year (still 1871), the Third Republic was formed and the Belle Époque (a kind of golden age) was ushered in. With it came the Eiffel Tower, impressionism, and the Moulin Rouge, and they partied like it was 1899 up until World War I began in 1914. An intense avant-garde scene sprang up between the wars—the arts boomed in Paris as musicians and artists from all over the world were drawn to the city. But the Depression and political unrest during the 1930s left France completely unprepared for World War

II. Hitler arrived with his army in June 1940, and they stayed until Allied troops liberated the city in August 1944.

The rest of the 20th century brought just one major uprising (in 1968) and lots of new *Grands Projects*, including the Pompidou Centre, the Louvre's new pyramid, the Opéra Bastille, and the Bibliothèque Nationale de France (the gigantic new library).

Tourists followed.

Left: Armistice Day, November 11, 1918. Above: The Liberation of Paris, August 1944.

THE INNOCENTS ABROAD

by Mark Twain

One night we went to the celebrated *Jardin Mabille,* but only staid a little while. We wanted to see some of this kind of Paris life, however, and therefore, the next night we went to a similar place of entertainment in a great garden in the suburb of Asnières. We went to the railroad depot, toward evening, and Ferguson got tickets for a second-class carriage. Such a perfect jam of people I have not often seen— but there was no noise, no disorder, no rowdyism. Some of the women and young girls that entered the train we knew to be of the *demi-monde,* but others we were not at all sure about.

The girls and women in our carriage behaved themselves modestly and becomingly, all the way out, except that they smoked. When we arrived at the garden in Asnières, we paid a franc or two admission, and entered a place which had flower-beds in it, and grass plats, and long, curving rows of ornamental shrubbery, with here and there a secluded bower convenient for eating ice-cream in. We moved along the sinuous gravel walks, with the great concourse of girls and young men, and suddenly a domed and filigreed white temple, starred over and over and over again with brilliant gas-jets, burst upon us like a fallen sun. Near by was a large, handsome house with its ample front illuminated in the same way, and above its roof floated the Star Spangled Banner of America.

Ferguson said an American—a New Yorker—kept the place, and was carrying on quite a stirring opposition to the *Jardin Mabille.*

Crowds, composed of both sexes

and nearly all ages, were frisking about the garden or sitting in the open air in front of the flag-staff and the temple, drinking wine and coffee, or smoking. The dancing had not begun, yet. The famous Blondin was going to perform on a tight-rope in another part of the garden. We went thither. Here the light was dim, and the masses of people were pretty closely packed together. And now I made a mistake which any donkey might make, but a sensible man never. I committed an error which I find myself repeating every day of my life.—Standing right before a young lady, I said—

"Dan, just look at this girl, how beautiful she is!"

"I thank you more for the evident sincerity of the compliment, sir, than for the extraordinary publicity you have given to it!" This in good, pure English.

We took a walk, but my spirits were very, very sadly dampened. I did not feel right comfortable for some time afterward. Why *will* people be so stupid as to suppose themselves the only foreigners among a crowd of ten thousand persons?

But Blondin came out shortly. He appeared on a stretched cable, far away above the sea of tossing hats and handkerchiefs, and in the glare of the hundreds of rockets that whizzed heavenward by him he looked like a wee insect. He balanced his pole and walked the length of his rope—two or three hundred feet; he came back and got a man and carried him across; he returned to the centre and danced a jig; and he finished by fastening to his person a thousand Roman candles, Catherine wheels, serpents and rockets of all manner of brilliant colors, setting them on fire all at once and walking and waltzing across his rope again in a blinding blaze of glory that lit up the garden and the people's faces like a great conflagration at midnight.

The dance had begun, and we adjourned to the temple. Within it was a drinking saloon; and all around it was a broad circular platform for the dancers. I backed up against the wall of the temple, and waited. Twenty sets formed, the music struck up, and then—I placed my hands before my face for very shame. But I looked through my fingers. They were dancing the renowned *"Can-can."* A handsome girl in the set before me tripped forward lightly to meet the opposite gentleman—tripped back again, grasped her dresses vigorously on both sides with her hands, raised them pretty high, danced an extraordinary jig that had more activity and exposure about it than any jig I ever saw before, and then, drawing her clothes still higher, she advanced gaily to the centre and launched a vicious kick full at her *vis-a-vis* that must infallibly have removed his nose if he had been seven feet high. It was a mercy he was only six.

That is the *can-can*. The idea of it is to dance as wildly, as noisily, as furiously as you can; expose yourself as much as possible if you are a woman; and kick as high as you can, no matter which sex you belong to. There is no word of exaggeration in this. Any of the staid, respectable, aged people who were there that night can testify to the truth of that statement. There were a good many such people present. I suppose French morality is not of that straight-laced description which is shocked at trifles.

I moved aside and took a general view of the *can-can*. Shouts, laughter, furious music, a bewildering chaos of darting and intermingling forms, stormy jerking and snatching of gay dresses, bobbing heads, flying arms, lightning-flashes of white-stockinged calves and dainty slippers in the air, and then a grand final rush, riot, a terrific hubbub and a wild stampede! Heavens! Nothing like it has been seen on earth since trembling Tam O'Shanter saw the devil and the witches at their orgies that stormy night in "Alloway's auld haunted kirk."

Museums

Les Hints

FOLLOW YOUR PASSIONS. There are over 200 museums and monuments in this city covering a wide range of interests, from impressionism to piles of bones. Even radium fans (Institut du Radium/Musée Curie) and those piqued by social security (Musée de l'Assistance Publique or the Public Assistance Museum) will find something to tickle their fancy.

BUY A MUSEUM PASS (Carte Musées et Monuments). More than 60 museums and monuments participate in this scheme, which is available at the ticket window of any of the museums or monuments and runs for two, four, or six days. If you plan to visit at least two museums a day you will save money. This is ideal for those who want to see the basics (since special exhibitions are not included in this pass). Other benefits include bypassing ticket lines and avoiding the confusing ticket choices available at each museum.

FREE DAYS. The permanent exhibits at the city of Paris museums are free to everyone, and all of the national museums and monuments are free the first Sunday of the month (except in the summer). But that means that you and everyone else (30,000 can show up at the Louvre on a slow day) might be craning their necks to see the *Mona Lisa*. Most museums are free to those 18 or under. Otherwise discounts are offered to students, those with large families, the disabled, and the unemployed.

OPEN? Most museums are closed either Monday or Tuesday; January 1, May 1, and Christmas Day are also big holidays. In general most museums open at 9 or 10 AM and close around 5 or 6 PM, but many stay open late once a week. Be sure to check for specific closings. In Paris anything can be closed on any day for any (or seemingly no) reason.

The Usual Suspects

CENTRE GEORGES POMPIDOU (almost always referred to as Beaubourg) (4è; Métro: Rambuteau, Hôtel de Ville, or Châtelet; place Georges Pompidou; +33 (0)1 44 78 12 33; cnac-gp.fr; closed Tuesday). One of the best collections of modern and contemporary art in Europe all wrapped up in a human-sized Habitrail. Special treat: lunch or dinner at Le Georges on the sixth level for the contoured aluminum sheeting and the panoramic views.

GRAND PALAIS (8è; Métro: Champs-Élysées-Clemenceau or Franklin D. Roosevelt; 3 avenue du Général Eisenhower; +33 (0)1 44 13 17 17; rmn.fr/galeriesnationalesdugrandpalais; closed Tuesday). Built for the Paris exhibition of 1900, this enormous glass building resembling a hothouse is *très cool*. Go to be surrounded by international art bathed in a stunning amount of space and light.

INVALIDES (7è; Métro: Latour-Maubourg; 129 rue de Grenelle; +33 (0)1 44 42 38 77; invalides.org; closed the first Monday of each month except July, August, September). Originally a hospital/housing for maimed and impoverished war veterans built under Louis XIV, it now holds a large military museum, a relief maps museum, a museum dedicated to the liberation of France after World War II, a magnificently domed church, and the body of Napoleon.

JEU DE PAUME (8è; Métro: Concorde; 1 place de la Concorde; +33 (0)1 47 03 12 50; jeudepaume.org; closed Monday). This tiny museum of photography and images from the 19th century to the present day (originally a handball court built by Napoleon III) provides the perfect antidote to the Louvre.

LOUVRE (1er; Métro: Palais Royal Musée du Louvre; louvre.fr; closed Tuesday). The *Mona Lisa, Venus de Milo, Winged Victory,* and 35,000 other treasures vie for attention at one of the oldest, largest galleries on the planet. If you're ready to know the secret, take the *Da Vinci Code* Soundwalk (audiotour) narrated by Jean Reno.

MUSÉE D'ORSAY (7è; Métro: Solférino; 1 rue de la Légion d'Honneur; +33 (0)1 40 49 48 14; musee-orsay.fr; closed Monday). Located in a former railway station, the Orsay houses a fabulous collection of mostly French art from 1848 to 1914. And although there is sculpture, photography, and even furniture (spectacular art nouveau), it is the incredible collection of impressionist masterpieces—by van Gogh, Monet, Renoir, and many others—that draws most to this museum.

L'ORANGERIE (1er; Métro: Concorde; Jardin des Tuileries; +33 (0)1 44 77 80 07; musee-orangerie.fr; closed Tuesday).

Eight panels of Monet's *Nymphéas,* giant paintings of his garden at Giverny, were given to the state as a gesture of peace—both military (after the Great War) and soul searching (humankind's need for inner tranquility in the modern world)—and are displayed in two rooms in this small museum devoted to modern art.

PANTHÉON (5è; Métro: Cardinal Lemoine). Here lie Voltaire, Zola, Hugo, and more in this former church turned *nécropole des grands hommes* (city of great—but dead—men) by the revolutionaries.

PÈRE LACHAISE (20è; Métro: Père Lachaise, Philippe August, or Gambetta; pere-lachaise.com). Two hundred years of the dead and the famous, from Balzac to Oscar Wilde. Bring a picnic lunch and spend the day.

SAINTE CHAPELLE (1er; Métro: Cité; 4 blvd du Palais; +33 (0)1 53 40 60 93). A jewel of Gothic architecture, this chapel was built by Louis IX (who later became Saint Louis) as a reliquary for Christ's crown of thorns and a piece of the cross. Visit on a sunny day to see the extraordinary stained-glass windows.

Les Artistes

CLAUDE MONET (Musée Marmottan-Monet) (16è; Métro: La Muette; 2 rue Louis-Boilly; +33 (0)1 44 96 50 33; marmottan.com; closed Monday). The largest collection of Monets in the world is enhanced by myriad Manets, Pissarros, Sisleys, and Renoirs donated by their personal physician, Dr. Georges de Bellio. This shrine to impressionism is housed in a former hunting lodge.

DALÍ (18è; Métro: Abbesses or Anvers; 11 rue Poulbot du Tertre; +33 (0)1 42 64 40 10; daliparis.com). This small homage to surrealist Dalí is almost like going into a Dalí fan's finished basement. It's a nice break from the hubbub of Montmartre, and the "art team" will help you make a purchase from the large gift shop.

DELACROIX (6è; Métro: Saint Germain des Prés; 6 rue de Furstenberg; +33 (0)1 44 41 86 50; musee-delacrox.fr; closed Tuesday). Paintings and memorabilia are on display in the French Romantic painter's last apartment and studio.

EDITH PIAF (11è; Métro: Ménilmontant; 5 rue Crespin du Gast; +33 (0)1 43 55 52 72; call for an appointment always, Monday–Wednesday 1–6 and Thursday 9–noon). Souvenirs of the singer nicknamed "Little Sparrow" fill the small apartment of Bernard Marchois, a devoted fan who, as a child, knew Piaf. Look for the tiny plaque outside the building that says LES AMIS DE EDITH PIAF, and bring a treat for the dog.

GUSTAVE MOREAU (9è; Métro: Trinité; +33 (0)1 48 74 38 50; www.musee-moreau.fr; closed Tuesday). The symbolist painter and teacher to Matisse (and Roualt, his star pupil) left his home and studio—along with many masterpieces—to France, and nothing has been changed there in over a century.

PICASSO MUSEUM (3è; Métro: Saint Paul; 5 rue de Thorigny; +33 (0)1 42 71 25 21; musee-picasso.fr; closed Tuesday). Just some of the artist's prolific works are displayed in this beautiful 17th-century mansion called Hôtel Salé (salted house) because it was once owned by a salt tax collector.

RODIN (7è; Métro: Varenne, Invalides, or Saint François Xavier; 79 rue de Varenne; +33 (0)1 44 18 61 10; musee-rodin.fr; closed Monday). Beside the masterpieces on display, like *The Kiss, The Thinker,* and *The Gates of Hell,* there are over 6,000 other sculptures in the collection housed in a château-like home surrounded by one of the lovliest gardens in the city.

Les Bibliophiles

BALZAC (16è; Métro: Passy; 47 rue Raynouard; +33 (0)1 55 74 41 80; balzac.paris.fr; closed Monday). Personal souvenirs, original manuscripts, and illustrations are arranged by theme throughout this five-room apartment—Balzac's last remaining residence in Paris.

VICTOR HUGO (4è; Métro: Bastille; 6 place des Vosges; +33 (0)1 42 72 10 16; musee-hugo.paris.fr; closed Monday). It's hard to believe that Victor Hugo could write of the wretchedness suffered in *Les Misérables* while looking out onto the Place des Voges, one of the most charming squares in town. Nonetheless the apartment he lived in for the last 16 years of his life has a nice collection of his drawings and books. Be sure to dine at any of the cafés on the square.

VIE ROMANTIQUE (Museum of Romanticism) (9è; Métro: Pigalle; 16 rue Chaptal; +33 (0)1 55 31 95 67; vie-romantique.paris.fr; closed Monday). This museum dedicated to life during Romanticism—the 19th-century anti-science-and-reason/pro-emotion movement—is really a tribute to George Sand. Reason could never explain how such a charming garden exists in the midst of seedy Pigalle.

For the Building Alone

CARNAVALET (3è; Métro: Chemin Vert or Saint Paul; 23, rue de Sévigné; +33 (0)1 44 59 58 58; carnavalet.paris.fr; closed Monday). Even if you think you're not interested in the history of Paris (from its origins through today), this museum is a must just to stand inside this 16th-century mini palace, former home to La Marquise de Sévigné.

COGNACQ-JAY (3è; Métro: Saint Paul; 8 rue Elzévir; +33 (0)1 40 27 07 21; cognacq-jay.paris.fr; closed Monday). Jewelry, sculpture, paintings, porcelains, furniture, and other objets d'art collected by the founders of the Samaritaine department store are housed in a 16th-century abode, l'hôtel Donon. In summer there is access to the garden.

JACQUEMART-ANDRÉ (8è; Métro: Miromesnil or Saint Philippe du Roule; 158 blvd Haussmann; +33 (0)1 45 62 11 59; musee-jacquemart-andre.com). French, Dutch, and Italian paintings, objets d'art, and furniture collected by the former owners of this magnificent Second Empire mansion.

Les Folies
(rough translation: madnesses)

BACCARAT (16è; Métro: Iéna; 11 place des États-Unis; +33 (0)1 40 22 11 00; closed Tuesday and Sunday). It's fitting that this homage to the sparkling crystal of Baccarat is located in the former home of socialite and eccentric patroness of the arts Marie-Laure de Noailles. Eat in the Cristal Room (redone by Philippe Starck) where Dalí, Cocteau, and Man Ray once supped with Marie, the great-great-great-granddaughter of the Marquis de Sade.

CATACOMBES (14è; Métro: Denfert Rochereau; +33 (0)1 43 22 47 63; closed Monday). The remains of six (or seven) million Parisians were removed from their previous "final" resting places, moved to the Catacombes, and stacked quite neatly within the 11,000 square meters of underground tunnels.

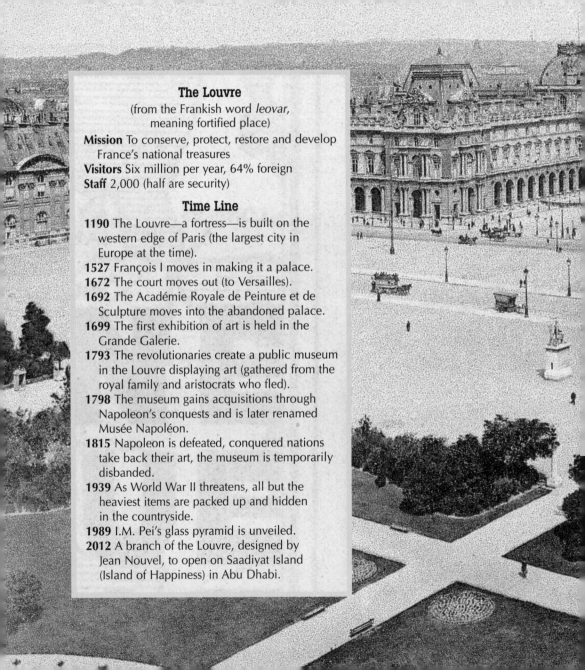

The Louvre

(from the Frankish word *leovar*,
meaning fortified place)

Mission To conserve, protect, restore and develop
France's national treasures

Visitors Six million per year, 64% foreign

Staff 2,000 (half are security)

Time Line

1190 The Louvre—a fortress—is built on the
western edge of Paris (the largest city in
Europe at the time).

1527 François I moves in making it a palace.

1672 The court moves out (to Versailles).

1692 The Académie Royale de Peinture et de
Sculpture moves into the abandoned palace.

1699 The first exhibition of art is held in the
Grande Galerie.

1793 The revolutionaries create a public museum
in the Louvre displaying art (gathered from the
royal family and aristocrats who fled).

1798 The museum gains acquisitions through
Napoleon's conquests and is later renamed
Musée Napoléon.

1815 Napoleon is defeated, conquered nations
take back their art, the museum is temporarily
disbanded.

1939 As World War II threatens, all but the
heaviest items are packed up and hidden
in the countryside.

1989 I.M. Pei's glass pyramid is unveiled.

2012 A branch of the Louvre, designed by
Jean Nouvel, to open on Saadiyat Island
(Island of Happiness) in Abu Dhabi.

ÉGOUTS DE PARIS (Sewer Museum) (7è; Métro: Alma Marceau; the entrance is on the Left Bank in front of 93 quai d'Orsay, look for the blue-and-white booth east of the Pont d'Alma; +33 (0)1 53 68 27 81; closed Thursday and Friday). Perhaps Paris's most . . . odious . . . attraction, it's still very historic, kind of interesting—and who can forget Jean Valjean carrying the practically dead Marius through the sewers to safety in *Les Mis?*

ÉROTISME (Erotic Museum) (18è; Métro: Blanche; 72 boulevard de Clichy; musee-erotisme.com). For those itching to get to a museum at 2 AM, this is probably the only choice in Paris, and the only one where you're allowed to ogle the nudes in more than an aesthetic way.

ÉVENTAIL (Decorative Fan Museum) (10è; Métro: Strasbourg Saint Denis; 2 blvd de Strasbourg; +33 (0)1 42 08 19 89; annehoguet.fr; open Monday–Wednesday). Master fan maker Anne Hoguet (the last in France) restores old fans, makes new ones, or answers questions in the museum attached to her workshop. There are nearly 1,000 fans on show from the 17th century onward.

JUDAÏSME (3è; Métro: Hôtel de Ville or Rambuteau; 71 rue du Temple; +33 (0)1 53 01 86 60; mahj.org; closed Saturday). The art and history of Judaism in France are highlighted through works of art and historic objects. The museum is housed in what was built as a 17th-century aristocratic residence.

MODE DE LA VILLE DE PARIS (Fashion of Paris) (16è; Métro: Iéna; 10 ave Pierre 1er de Serbie; +33 (0)1 56 52 86 00; galliera.paris.fr; open only during specific exhibits, and closed Monday). Ninety thousand pieces of couture—both high and low—from the 17th to the 20th centuries are in the collection.

MODE ET TEXTILE (Fashion and Fabric) (1er; Métro: Palais Royal–Musée du Louvre, Tuileries, or Pyramides; 107 rue de Rivoli; +33 (0)1 44 55 57 50; lesartsdecoratifs.fr; closed Monday). Sixteen thousand outfits, 35,000 accessories, and 30,000 different fabrics from the ordinary to Gaultier are housed in this section of the Louvre. Put on your best Lacroix and dive in.

MONNAIE (6è; Métro: Pont Neuf; 11 quai de Conti; +33 (0)1 40 46 57 09; monnaiedeparis.fr; closed Monday). A museum for the coin collector displaying cash from Renaissance times to the euro.

MOYEN-AGE THERMES DE CLUNY (Middle Ages and Gallo-Roman Baths) (5è; Métro: Cluny La Sorbonne; 6 place Paul Painlevé; +33 (0)1 53 73 78 00; musee-moyenage.fr; closed Tuesday). Beside the frigidarium and caldarium you'll find the ancient mosaic *Love Rides a Dolphin* and tapestries from the Middle Ages housed in Roman baths. The 15th-century Cluny Abbey is here too.

PALAIS DE TOKYO (16è; Métro: Iéna; 13 ave du Président Wilson; +33 (0)1 47 23 38 86; palaisdetokyo.com; closed Monday). Built as an exhibition space for a 1937 fair, this art deco bauble has been transformed into Paris's most contemporary art space—the cutting edge is on view here until midnight. They have a great book store too.

PARFUM-FRAGONARD (Perfume Museum) (9è; Métro: Opéra; 9 rue Scribe; +33 (0)1 47 42 04 56; fragonard.com). Take a guided tour through the history and manufacturing process of perfume. Best are the beautiful flacons from ancient to modern times.

MUSÉE DE LA POUPÉE (Doll Museum) (3è; Métro: Rambuteau; Impasse Berthaud, a little alley near 22 rue Beaubourg; +33 (0)1 42 72 73 11; museedelapoupeeparis.com; closed Monday). From bisque-headed fashion dolls of the 19th century to Barbie, this museum is for doll lovers of all ages. And if your doll is sick or maimed—whether made of bisque, celluloid, or rhodoïd—the on-site doll hospital will make it all better.

YVES SAINT LAURENT (Fondation Pierre Bergé–Yves Saint Laurent) (16è; Métro: Alma Marceau; 1 rue Léonce Reynaud; +33 (0)1 44 31 64 00; fondation-pb-ysl.net; open Monday–Friday). More than just rooms to show Saint Laurent or other designers' fashions, the galleries at the Maison Yves Saint Laurent plan exhibitions of paintings, photographs, and drawings too.

ARRONDISSEMENT
2ÈME

Between the bankers and stockbrokers found working and going to meetings around the Bourse (the stock market) and the prostitutes arranging meetings around the rue Saint Denis, the second arrondissement is mostly business . . . and a little retail. The Passage du Caire built in 1799 was the first of a series of glass-covered shopping streets, called *passages couverts,* that were popular in the early 19th century before sidewalks made shopping on the street feasible. The streets around the passage (rue d'Aboukir, d'Alexandrie, du Nil) are signs of the wave of Egyptomania that swept Paris after Napoleon's Egyptian campaign, which, although a disaster militarily, brought home a treasure trove of artistic and architectural ideas. Look for the three images of the cow-eared Egyptian god Hathor decorating buildings on Place du Caire.

On Saturday the pedestrian rue Montorgueil becomes the neighborhood's outdoor supermarket. Look for farmers selling their wares while giving detailed advice on when exactly to eat a certain cheese, while fishmongers call out the day's specials.

"Lucky Lindy"
Charles A. Lindbergh
(1902–1974)

The American pilot gained sudden worldwide fame in 1927 after making the first solo, non-stop transatlantic flight from New York to Paris. A true American hero, Lindbergh and his family ended up moving to Europe (England and France) to avoid the ceaseless public attention resulting from the kidnapping and death of his eldest son and the sensational trial that followed.

Later in life he lived in Connecticut and worked as a consultant to the US Air Force and Pan American Airways.

I'm still flying at four thousand feet when I see it, that scarcely perceptible glow, as though the moon had rushed ahead of schedule. Paris is rising over the edge of the earth. It's almost thirty-three hours from my take-off on Long Island. As minutes pass, myriad pin points of light emerge, a patch of starlit earth under a starlit sky—the lamps of Paris—straight lines of lights, curving lines of lights, squares of lights, black spaces in between. Gradually avenues, parks, and buildings take outline form; and there, far below, a little offset from the center, is a column of lights pointing upward, changing angles as I fly—the Eiffel Tower. I circle once above it, and turn northeastward toward Le Bourget. —CHARLES A. LINDBERGH

Lindbergh Does It! To Paris In 33 1/2 Hours; Flies 1,000 Miles Through Snow And Sleet; Cheering French Carry Him Off Field

—*New York Times* headline, May 22, 1927

GENTLEMEN PREFER BLONDES

by Anita Loos

April 27th:

Paris is devine. I mean Dorothy and I got to Paris yesterday, and it really is devine. Because the French are devine. Because when we were coming off the boat, and we were coming through the customs, it was quite hot and it seemed to smell quite a lot and all the French gentlemen in the customs, were squealing quite a lot. So I looked around and I picked out a French gentleman who was really in a very gorgeous uniform and he seemed to be a very, very important gentleman and I gave him twenty francs worth of French money and he was very very gallant and he knocked everybody else down and took our bags right through the custom. Because I really think that twenty Francs is quite cheap for a gentleman that has got on at least $100 worth of gold braid on his coat alone, to speak nothing of his trousers.

I mean the French gentlemen always seem to be squealing quite a lot, especially taxi drivers when they only get a small size yellow dime called a 'fifty santeems' for a tip. But the good thing about French gentlemen is that every time a French gentleman starts in to squeal, you can always stop him with five francs, no matter who he is. I mean it is so refreshing to listen to a French gentleman stop squeaking, that it would really be quite a bargain even for ten francs.

So we came to the Ritz Hotel and

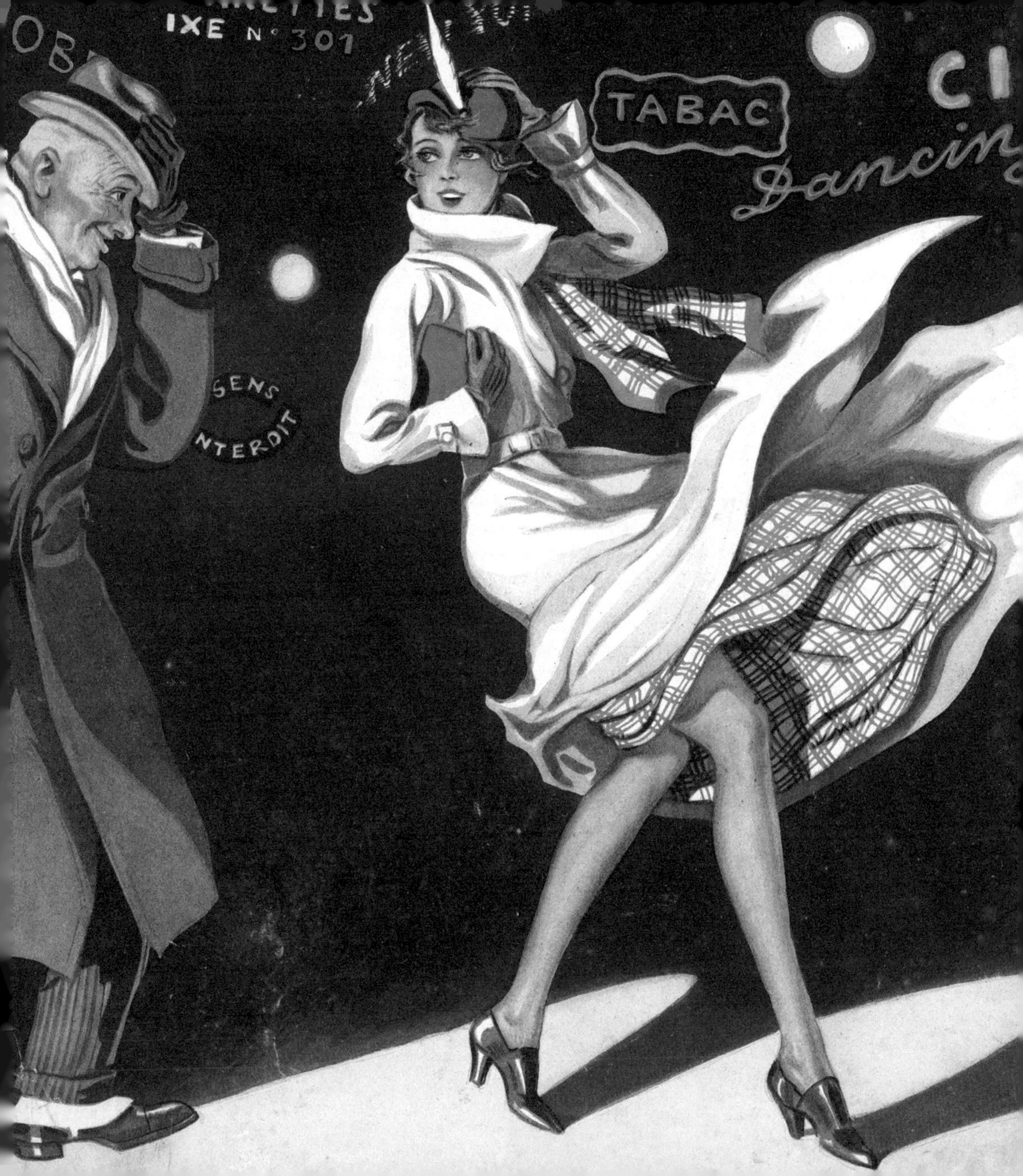
IXE N° 301
TABAC
SENS

the Ritz Hotel is devine. Because when a girl can sit in a delightful bar and have delicious champagne cocktails and look at all the important French people in Paris, I think it is devine. I mean when a girl can sit there and look at the Dolly sisters and Pearl White and Maybelle Gilman Corey, and Mrs. Nash, it is beyond worlds. Because when a girl looks at Mrs. Nash and realizes what Mrs. Nash has got out of gentlemen, it really makes a girl hold her breath.

And when a girl walks around and reads all of the signs with all of the famous historical names it really makes you hold your breath. Because when Dorothy and I went on a walk, we only walked a few blocks but in only a few blocks we read all of the famous historical names, like Coty and Cartier and I knew we were seeing something educational at last and our whole trip was not a failure. I mean I really try to make Dorothy get educated and have reverance. So when we stood at the corner of a place called the

Place Vandome, if you turn your back on a monument they have in the middle and look up, you can see none other than Coty's sign. So I said to Dorothy, does it not really give you a thrill to realize that that is the historical spot where Mr. Coty makes all the perfume? So then Dorothy said that she supposed Mr. Coty came to Paris and he smelled Paris and he realized that something had to be done. So Dorothy will really never have any reverance.

So then we saw a jewelry store and we saw some jewelry in the window and it really seemed to be a very very great bargain but the price marks all had francs on them and Dorothy and I do not seem to be mathematical enough to tell how much francs is in money. So we went in and asked and it seems it was only 20 dollars and it seems it is not diamonds but it is a thing called "paste" which is the name of a word which means imitations. So Dorothy said "paste" is the name of the word a girl ought to do to a gentleman that handed her one. I mean I would really be embarrassed, but the gentleman did not seem to understand Dorothy's english.

So it really makes a girl feel depressed to think a girl could not tell that it was nothing but an imitation. I mean a gentleman could deceeve a girl because he could give her a present and it would only be worth 20 dollars. So when Mr. Eisman comes to Paris next week, if he wants to make me a present I will make him take me along with him because he is really quite an inveteran bargain hunter at heart. So the gentleman at the jewelry store said that quite a lot of famous girls in Paris had imitations of all their jewelry and they put the jewelry in the safe and they really wore the imitations, so they could wear it and have a good time. But I told him I thought that any girl who was a lady would not even think of having such a good time that she did not remember to hang on to her jewelry.

So then we went back to the Ritz and unpacked our trunks with the aid of really a delightful waiter who brought us up some delicious luncheon and who is called Leon and who speaks english almost like an American and who Dorothy and I talk to quite a lot. So Leon said that we ought not to stay around the Ritz all of the time, but we really ought to see Paris. So Dorothy said she would go down in the lobby and meet some gentleman to show us Paris. So in a couple of minutes she called up on the telephone from the lobby and she said "I have got a French bird down here who is a French title nobleman, who is called a veecount so come on down." So I said "How did a Frenchman get into the Ritz." So Dorothy said "He came in to get out of the rain and he has not noticed that it is stopped." So I said "I suppose you have picked up something without taxi fare as usual. Why did you not get an American gentleman who always have money?" So Dorothy said she thought a French gentleman had ought to know Paris better. So I said

"He does not even know it is not raining." But I went down.

So the veecount was really delightful after all. So then we rode around and we saw Paris and we saw how devine it really is. I mean the Eyefull Tower is devine and it is much more educational than the London Tower, because you can not even see the London Tower if you happen to be two blocks away. But when a girl looks at the Eyefull Tower she really knows she is looking at something. And it would even be very difficult not to notice the Eyefull Tower.

So then we went to a place called the Madrid to tea and it really was devine. I mean we saw the Dolley Sisters and Pearl White and Mrs. Corey and Mrs. Nash all over again.

So then we went to dinner and then we went to Momart and it really was devine because we saw them all over again. I mean in Momart they have genuine American jazz bands and quite a lot of New York people which we knew and you really would think you were in New York and it was devine. So we came back to the Ritz quite late. So Dorothy and I had quite a little quarrel because Dorothy said that when we were looking at Paris I asked the French veecount what was the name of the unknown soldier who is buried under quite a large monument. So I said I really did not mean to ask him, if I did, because what I did mean to ask him was, what was the name of his mother because it is always the mother of a dead soldier that I always seem to think about more than the dead soldier that has died.

So the French veecount is going to call up in the morning but I am not going to see him again. Because French gentlemen are really quite deceeving. I mean they take you to quite cute places and they make you feel quite good about yourself and you really seem to have a delightful time but when you get home and come to think it all over, all you have got is a fan that only cost 20 francs and a doll that they gave you

away for nothing in a restaurant. I mean a girl has to look out in Paris, or she would have such a good time in Paris that she would not get anywheres. So I really think that American gentlemen are the best after all, because kissing your hand may make you feel very very good but a diamond and safire bracelet lasts forever. Besides, I do not think that I ought to go out with any gentlemen in Paris because Mr. Eisman will be here next week and he told me that the only kind of gentlemen he wants to me to go out with are intelectual gentlemen who are good for a girl's brains. So I really do not seem to see many gentlemen around the Ritz who seem to look like they would be good for a girls brains. So tomorrow we are going to go shopping and I suppose it would really be to much to expect to find a gentleman who would look to Mr. Eisman like he was good for a girls brains and at the same time he would like to take us shopping. 🏛

Le Shopping

Shopping is literally everywhere in Paris. One of the most important things to know about shopping in Paris is that twice a year (in January and July) everything in the city goes on sale (by government mandate!) for around six weeks. Here are some of the basics.

Les Grands Magasins

Department stores was invented in Paris toward the end of the 19th century, and *les grand magasins* is what Parisians call them. Bon Marché, Galeries Lafayette, and Printemps, along with Samaritaine (closed for renovations until further notice) make up the four main stores in this grand shopping mecca.

BON MARCHÉ (7è; Métro: Vaneau or Sèvres Babylone; 24 rue de Sèvres; +33 (0)1 44 39 80 00). Baubles, buttons, and boas are for sale in the old-fashioned haberdashery in this, the first department store in the world. Be sure to stop in the Grand Épicerie (food shop) nearby at number 38 rue de Sèvres, where you can pick up horse milk, among other delicacies.

GALERIES LAFAYETTE (9è; 40 blvd Haussmann; +33 (0)1 42 82 34 56). There is nothing like the glass domed cupola hanging over the layer-cake-like balconies of the main room in this store. Even if you are not a shopper, stop by, along with the 100,000 others each day, to take it all in.

PRINTEMPS (9è; 64 blvd Haussmann; +33 (0)1 42 82 57 87). Maybe not as glamorous as Bon Marché, but it hosts the largest beauty department in the world, and the ninth-floor cafeteria has an amazing 360-degree view of Paris.

Luxury Goods

France is renowned for its luxury goods, and here are two fabulous areas where deluxe is de rigueur. Avenue Montaigne, in the eighth arrondissement—which, along with Avenue George V and the Champs-Élysées, makes up the Triangle d'Or (the golden triangle)—is the best place to start. High fashion (Dior, Dolce & Gabbana, Chanel), jewelry (Bulgari, Harry Winston), and luxury hotels (the Plaza Athénée) are all within minutes of one another. Next, head to

the romantic arches of the Palais Royal in the first arrondissement to buy a Serge Luton fragrance (Les Salons du Palais Royal Shiseido, 142 galerie de Valois), only available at the shop (some fragrances are not sold anywhere else or even shipped outside Europe); a classic little black dress at La Petite Robe Noire (125 galerie de Valois); or a marionette theater (La Boutique du Palais Royal; 9 rue de Beaujolais).

Street Markets

There are several food markets open throughout the city during the week. They are where you will find incredibly fresh food, and make the perfect place to catch Parisians in action, both buyers and sellers, like the grizzled fishmonger yelling out how great his halibut is.

RUE D'ALIGRE (12è; Métro: Ledru-Rollin; Tuesday–Sunday mornings). One of the best-priced and more exotic markets due to the mix of African, Asian, and Caribbean neighbors.

RUE DE BUCI (6è; Métro: Mabillon; Tuesday–Sunday). Fresh fruit and veg and a bunch of cafés and boutiques to stop in after shopping.

FLOWERS and BIRDS (4è; Métro: Cité; flowers 8–7 every day except Sunday; birds on Sunday). Flowers during the week, and birds and everything you'd ever need to feed Tweety can be found here on Sunday.

RUE MONTORGUEIL (2è; Métro: Les Halles; Sunday morning). The only market left from the original Les Halles. Vendors have been shucking their oysters on this street for a millennium.

RUE MOUFFETARD (5è; Métro: Termes; Tuesday–Saturday and Sunday morning). One of the most famous food markets in Paris, and perhaps the most picturesque too.

Flea Markets

The granddaddy of all flea markets is Paris's Saint Ouen Flea Market also known as Le Marché aux Puces (Métro: Porte de Cligancourt; parispuces.com). Huge and popular, open only Saturday, Sunday, and Monday.

The Marché aux Puces de la Porte Vanves (Métro: Porte de Vanves; pucesdeparis-portedevanves.com) has over 350 stalls selling everything from party accessories to pop art every Saturday and Sunday.

ARRONDISSEMENT 3ÈME

Rich from the Crusades, it was the Knights Templar who originally settled this neighborhood during the Middle Ages, draining this part of what is now known as le Marais (the swamp) and building their own little walled village here. Today only the narrow medieval streets (Temple and Vielle du Temple) remind one of the Templars, whose buildings were razed and whose members were burned at the stake.

During the 17th century this neighborhood became home to many aristocrats who followed King Henri IV to the area. And although they later abandoned the Marais when the court moved to Versailles, many of their mansions can still be seen and even visited. Two of the most accessible are the Hôtel Salé, which belonged to a wealthy salt tax collector (now the Musée Picasso), and the Hôtel Carnavalet (now the Musée Carnavalet), former residence of the Marquise de Sévigné.

This, the quiet end of the Marais, is dotted with deconstructed art galleries, trendy clothing boutiques, Chinese wholesale shops, and some of the oldest residential buildings in Paris. Many apartments— these days filled with "bobos" (bohemian bourgeois), a trendy group of working artistic types—still have the old timber beams. Two often overlooked museums in the neighborhood are the Musée des Arts et Métiers (science and gadgets) and the tiny and well-hidden Musée de la Poupée (doll museum).

Café Society

The café is where the Parisian goes (often after work) to have one coffee or one drink, smoke dozens of cigarettes, and gab—for hours. He does not have two drinks, he does not eat (even though there is food available), and the waiter never bothers him to move along.

Last year when I was sitting at my favorite café minding my own business (and my neighbor's business . . . and his neighbor's business a little), the bells began ringing at Saint Gervais, a medieval church across the street, and I realized a wedding was about to begin. But before it did, members of the wedding party started to gather all around me at the café to chat before the ceremony. There was the beautiful bride thin as a rail in her mini-ish dress, the angular groom with his blond hair pulled back to form a perfect ponytail, her parents dressed to the nines, and his grandmother so elegantly attired in her pin-striped Yves Saint Laurent pantsuit circa 1970. That's what the Parisian café is really for . . . to sip your *café crème* and people-watch.

Un Café S'il Vous Plaît

Ordering a *café* will get you an espresso, *café crème* is an espresso with milk, a *noisette* is espresso with just a dash of milk, and *café americain* is an espresso with lots of water in it (closest to American-style coffee). *Café serré* is a dense *café* Italian-style, and if you have a trying day ahead you might order *café calva* (as the local workers do) with Calvados (an apple brandy). *Déca* is decaf.

Of the hundreds of cafés in Paris, here are a few of the more famous:

LES DEUX MAGOTS (6è; Métro: Saint Germain des Prés; 6 place Saint Germain des Prés), named for the two Chinese figurines left over from the shop that was once housed here. *Who hung here:* Philosophers, writers, and artists including Picasso who, they say, thought up Cubism on the terrace. *Today's regulars:* Some art, fashion, and political types, mostly American tourists.

CAFÉ DE FLORE (6è; Métro: Saint Germain des Prés; 172 blvd Saint Germain). Rival to neighbor Les Deux Magots. Philosophy was deeply discussed along the boulevard here in the early 20th century.

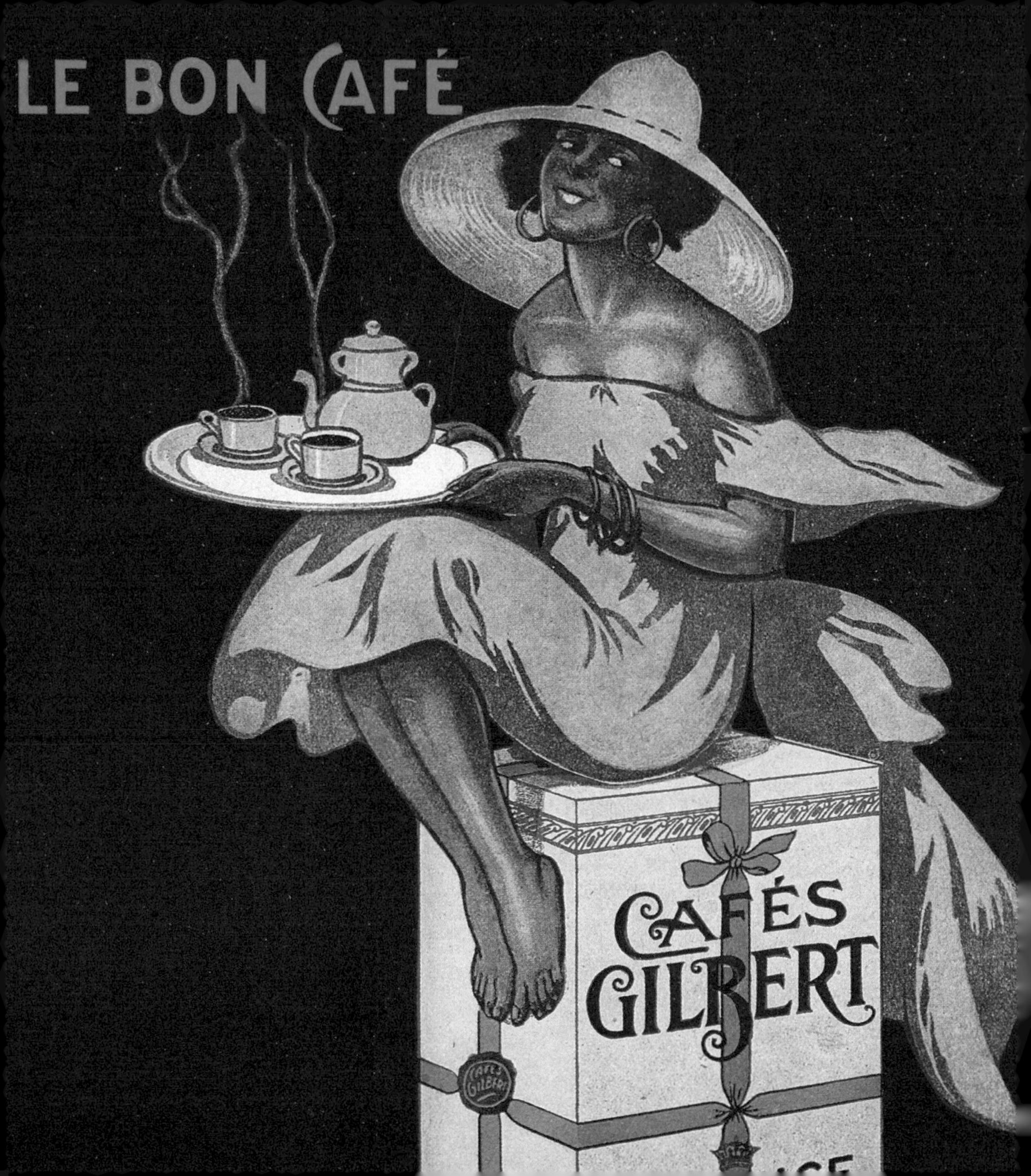
LE BON CAFÉ
CAFÉS
GILBERT

Who hung here: Jean-Paul Sartre and Simone de Beauvoir. *Today's regulars:* Sofia Coppola (during the filming of *Marie Antoinette*), sometimes Karl Lagerfeld, rumors of Johnny Depp, lots of American tourists.

BRASSERIE LIPP (6è; Métro: Saint Germain des Prés; 151 blvd Saint Germain; +33 (0)1 45 48 53 91). Just across the street from Les Deux Magots and Café de Flore, this deco brasserie is very like a café (history- and hangout-wise). They serve food, but lots of gabbing has gone on here too. *Who hung here:* Proust, Hemingway, lots of artists. *Today's regulars:* Politicians, newspeople, Arnold Schwarzenegger (when he owned nearby Planet Hollywood), and tourists.

CAFÉ DE LA PAIX (9è; Métro: Opéra; 12 blvd des Capucines). Designed by Charles Garnier, the man who brought you the delicious Opéra across the street. *Who hung here:* Oscar Wilde, Josephine Baker, Emile Zola. *Today's regulars:* Tourists eating before and after the opera.

LE PROCOPE (6è; Métro: Odeon; 13 rue de l'Ancienne Comédie; +33 (0)1 40 46 79 00) is a café/bar/restaurant; it is thought to be one of the oldest operating in the world. *Who hung here:* Ben Franklin, Napoleon, Balzac, Victor

Hugo. *Today's regulars:* Writers, businessmen, history buffs.

CAFÉ BEAUBOURG (4è; Métro: Châtelet or Rambuteau; 100 rue Saint Martin; +33 (0)1 48 87 63 96). Next to the huge pedestrian plaza of the Pompidou (Beaubourg) Museum is this ultra-hip café owned by the Costes brothers. *Who hung here:* The cool, the trendy, the tired from Beaubourg. *Today's regulars:* The cool, the trendy, local gallery workers, the tired from Beaubourg.

My Favorite

L'ETINCELLE (4è; Métro: Hôtel de Ville; 42 bis rue de Rivoli). *Today's regulars:* Me and the occasional wedding party.

ARRONDISSEMENT 4EME

The Iron Age Parisii (a Celtic tribe) who settled by the Seine around 250 BC are long gone from this neighborhood. Still, this tiny arrondissement is rich in what makes Paris Paris: Notre Dame, Sainte Chappelle, the Île de la Cité, the Île Saint Louis, and the Hôtel de Ville are just some of the well-known sites.

Known as le Marais (referring to "the swamp" that was drained centuries ago), this is one of the oldest and most diverse parts of town in terms of street layout and medieval buildings. To be surrounded by 17th-century Paris, just step onto the charming Île St. Louis. For the most part there are no grand boulevards, vast perspectives, or symmetry—the Place des Vosges, Paris's oldest square, being an exception. There you will find lots of symmetry, along with the Maison Victor Hugo, the great writer's last residence.

The people of le Marais are diverse too. Although by no means a ghetto, you'll find a large gay population, many gay bars and restaurants (that are well filled with straight people), and a distinctly Jewish area centered on the rue des Rosiers, where Orthodox Jews settled after being expelled from Paris in the 12th century (this was out of town back then). Chez Marianne (2 rue des Hospitalières–Saint Gervais) has extraordinarily fresh and delicious falafel, and an art nouveau synagogue (10 rue Pavée) designed by Hector Guimard (chandeliers, benches, and all) is here.

The Last Time I Saw Paris

BY OSCAR HAMMERSTEIN II

I'll think of happy hours,
And people who shared them
Old women, selling flowers, in markets at dawn
Children who applauded, Punch and Judy in the park
And those who danced at night
and kept Paris bright
'Til the town went dark.

Besides being the home address of Quasimodo—literature's best-known hunchback and bell ringer—Notre Dame is also home to Point Zéro, the center of Paris. Arguably the most beautiful Gothic cathedral on the planet, Notre Dame (out of necessity, since the walls began to bow as they grew taller and taller) was one of the first to use the flying buttress. And what took almost 200 years to build was nearly lost many times over the next 700 years. In fact, it's miraculous that the building even exists at all considering its history:

> And the cathedral was not only company for him, it was the universe; nay, more, it was Nature itself. He never dreamed that there were other hedgerows than the stained-glass windows in perpetual bloom; other shade than that of the stone foliage always budding, loaded with birds in the thickets of Saxon capitals; other mountains than the colossal towers of the church; or other oceans than Paris roaring at their feet.
>
> —Victor Hugo, *Notre Dame de Paris,* 1831

- Overtaken by rioting Huguenots (displeased with the Council of Trent) in 548.
- "Redecorated" by Louis XIV and XV (who destroyed tombs and removed stained glass).
- Plundered and rededicated to "the Cult of Reason" by revolutionaries in 1793 (who replaced the Virgin Mary with Lady Liberty).
- Almost torn down by city bureaucrats (until Victor Hugo's 1831 novel *Notre Dame de Paris,* starring Quasimodo, brought awareness to its plight).
- Set afire by the Communards in 1871.
- *Slightly* shelled in 1914.

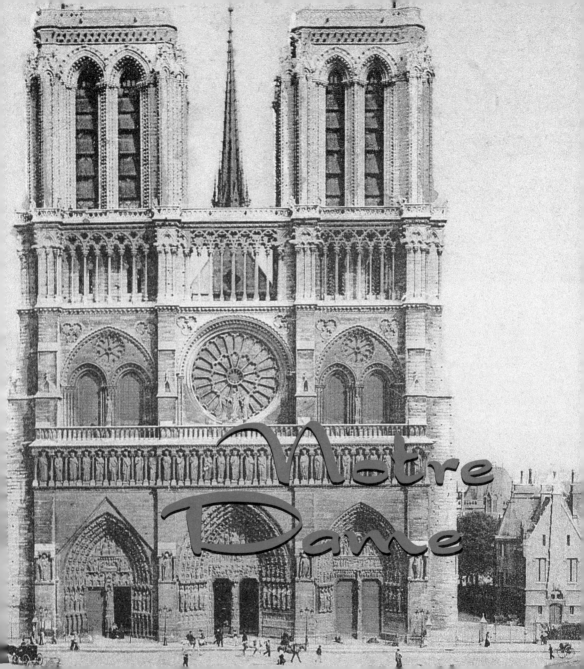
Notre Dame

THE CONCIERGE OF NOTRE DAME

From The Secret Paris of the 30s

by Brassaï

One winter day in 1932, I got the urge to climb to the top of Notre-Dame at night.

"The concierge is on the second floor," they told me at the entrance. So I climbed up—200 steps—and between two groups of tourists, I confronted the woman who watched over Notre-Dame.

"Climb up here at night, sir? It's unheard of! It's out of the question. We're a national museum, just like the Louvre. And we close at five!"

I discreetly slipped her a bill.

"I shouldn't let you, sir! It's wrong! Even though I am very badly paid . . .

and I have heart trouble, and I'm short of breath . . . Imagine! Two hundred steps every time I come up, and such steps! I was young once, not so fat, and I climbed up here twice a day. Now I come up in the morning and bring my lunch, and I don't go back until evening . . . Coming up here twice in one day will be hard on me, very hard. But you're generous, and you love Notre-Dame! I'll do it for you . . . a favor I've never done for anyone else . . . Only promise me not to use any light, not even a match. We're right across from the Préfecture de Police. The slightest glimmer would be suspi-

cious. I could lose my job over it . . ."

I reassure her. Taking advantage of a lull while the tourists moved off, the capacious woman continued in a low voice: "Look." With her plump finger, she indicated a particular place down in the square. "You see the third lamp-post on the right? Be there at ten tonight. I don't want you to come looking for me in the concierge's loge."

I was under the lamppost on the stroke of ten, and through the November mist, I saw a voluminous silhouette emerge from the Rue du Cloître-Notre-Dame and come toward me.

"Follow me," the concierge whispered in a muffled voice.

We were like conspirators in a Victor Hugo novel. She carried a bunch of keys, and with them she opened the heavy door.

We climbed the spiral staircase. It was totally dark; the climb lasted

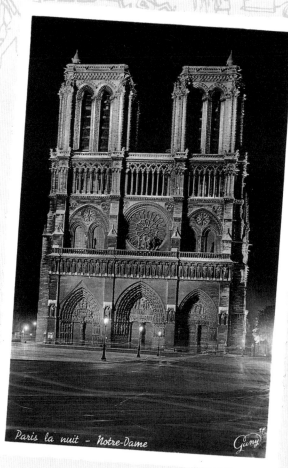

Paris la nuit - Notre-Dame

an eternity. At last, we reached the open platform. Completely out of breath, my accomplice collapsed into her chair. Impatient, enraptured, I ran beside the balustrade. It was more beautiful than I had imagined! The dark, indefinable shapes were black as night, the fog over Paris was milk white! Scarcely discernible, the Hôtel-Dieu, the Tour Saint-Jacques, the Quartier Latin, the Sorbonne, were luminous and somber shapes . . . Paris was ageless, bodiless . . . Present and past, history and legend, intermingled. Atop this cathedral, I expected to meet Quasimodo the bell-ringer around some corner, and later, upon descending into the city, I would certainly pass Verlaine and François Villon, the Marquis de Sade, Gérard de Nerval, Restif de la Bretonne.

"It's marvelous, marvelous," I kept exclaiming to myself.

"Isn't it, sir?" the fat woman replied, brimming with pride at being the concierge of Notre-Dame. "You don't see that anywhere else . . . We're at the heart of Paris . . . It beats the Eiffel Tower, doesn't it?"

But I had to get to the very top.

"Climb on up if you want, sir. I'll stay here; I can't go any farther . . . I trust you. Go on. You won't steal the towers of Notre-Dame."

So up I climbed, still in complete darkness. I mounted the 378 steps. Coming out at the top, I saw behind the cathedral's spire the Seine glittering like a curved sword. Suddenly my foot brushed against something soft. I bent down, and beneath my fingers, numb from the cold of that November night, I felt the feathers of a dead pigeon. A dead pigeon, still warm . . .

ARRONDISSEMENT 5ÈME

This classic Parisian neighborhood is what many have in mind when the Left Bank, or Rive Gauche is mentioned. Bustling with students browsing the bookstores or shopping along Boulevard Saint Michel and tourists eating at very bad Greek restaurants lining charming medieval streets, the neighborhood is also home to the Panthéon (housing the dead and the famous), Shakespeare and Company (the well-known English-language bookshop), and la Tour d'Argent, a very old (more than 400 years) formal French eatery overlooking Notre Dame.

What is now known as the Latin Quarter was once the center of ancient Roman Paris (or Lutetia as the Romans called it—Lutèce in French); they left behind the Thermes de Cluny (baths) and Arènes de Lutèce (an amphitheater). The neighborhood nickname did not arrive with the Romans, however. It came much later—in the 13th century—when Robert de Sorbon founded a school that attracted a multitude of foreign students who used Latin (the language of scholarly pursuits) to communicate.

To the east is the lively rue Mouffetard ("la Mouffe" to the locals), originally the road to Rome, now a daily market, and the lovely Jardin des Plantes—originally a medicinal garden started by Louix XIII's doctor—that provides a nice escape from the city buzz.

One of the neighborhood's most dramatic—if fictional—residents was the poor consumptive seamstress Mimi of *La Bohème* fame, who, lived, loved, and coughed in a roof-top garret here.

So, this is Gay Paree... Come along with me we're stepping out to see the Latin Quarter

Program

Latin Quarter

I Love Paris

BY COLE PORTER

I love Paris in the spring time,
I love Paris in the fall,
I love Paris in the winter, when it drizzles,
I love Paris in the summer, when it sizzles,

I love Paris ev'ry moment,
Ev'ry moment of the year,
I love Paris, why, oh why do I love Paris?
Because my love is near.

LES MISÉRABLES

by Victor Hugo

Fantine was one of those beings which are brought forth from the heart of the people. Sprung from the most unfathomable depths of social darkness, she bore on her brow the mark of the anonymous and unknown. She was born at M—— on M——. Who were her parents? None could tell, she had never known either father or mother. She was called Fantine—why so? because she had never been known by any other name. At the time of her birth, the Directory was still in existence. She could have no family name, for she had no family; she could have no baptismal name, for then there was no church. She was named after the pleasure of the first passer-by who found her, a mere infant, straying barefoot in the streets. She received a name as she received the water from the clouds on her head when it rained. She was called little Fantine. Nobody knew anything more of her. Such was the manner in which this human being had come into life. At the age of ten, Fantine left the city and went to service among the farmers of the suburbs. At fifteen, she came to Paris, to "seek her fortune." Fantine was beautiful and remained pure as long as she could. She was a pretty blonde with fine teeth. She had gold and pearls for her dowry; but the gold was on her head and the pearls in her mouth.

She worked to live; then, also to live, for the heart too has its hunger, she loved.

She loved Tholomyès.

To him, it was an amour; to her a

passion. The streets of the Latin Quarter, which swarm with students and grisettes, saw the beginning of this dream. Fantine, in those labyrinths of the hill of the Pantheon, where so many ties are knotted and unloosed, long fled from Tholomyès, but in such a way as always to meet him again. There is a way of avoiding a person which resembles a search. In short, the eclogue took place.

Blacheville, Listolier, and Fameuil formed a sort of group of which Tholomyès was the head. He was the wit of the company.

Tholomyès was an old student of the old style; he was rich, having an income of four thousand francs—a splendid scandal on the Montagne Sainte-Geneviève. He was a good liver, thirty years old, and ill preserved. He was wrinkled, his teeth were broken, and he was beginning to show signs of baldness, of which he said, gaily: *The head at thirty, the knees at forty.* His digestion was not good, and he had a weeping eye. But in proportion as his youth died out, his gaiety increased; he replaced his teeth by jests, his hair by joy, his health by irony, and his weeping eye was always laughing. He was dilapidated, but covered with flowers. His youth, decamping long before its time, was beating a retreat in good order, bursting with laughter, and displaying no loss of fire. He had had a piece refused at the Vaudeville; he made verses now and then on any subject; moreover, he doubted everything with an air of superiority—a great power in the eyes of the weak. So, being bald and ironical, he was the chief. Can the word *iron* be the root from which irony is derived?

One day, Tholomyès took the other three aside, and said to them with an oracular gesture:

"For nearly a year, Fantine, Dahlia, Zéphine, and Favourite have been asking us to give them a surprise; we have solemnly promised them one. They are constantly reminding us of it, me especially. Just as the old women at Naples cry to Saint January, '*Faccia gialluta, fa o miracolo,* yellow face, do your miracle,' our pretty ones are always saying: 'Tholomyès, when are you going to be delivered of your surprise?' At the same time our parents are writing for us. Two birds with one stone. It seems to me the time has come. Let us talk it over."

Upon this, Tholomyès lowered his voice, and mysteriously articulated something so ludicrous that a prolonged and enthusiastic giggling arose from the four throats at once, and Blacheville exclaimed: "What an idea!"

An ale-house, filled with smoke, was before them; they entered, and the rest of their conference was lost in its shade.

The result of this mystery was a brilliant pleasure party, which took place on the following Sunday, the four young men inviting the four young girls.

JOYOUS END OF JOY

The girls, left alone, leaned their elbows on the window sills in couples, and chattered together, bending their heads and speaking from one window to the other.

They saw the young men go out of Bombarda's, arm in arm; they turned round, made signals to them laughingly, then disappeared in the dusty Sunday crowd which takes possession of the Champs-Elysées once a week.

"Do not be long!" cried Fantine.

"What are they going to bring us?" said Zéphine.

"Surely something pretty," said Dahlia.

"I hope it will be gold," resumed Favourite.

They were soon distracted by the stir on the water's edge, which they distinguished through the branches of the tall trees, and which diverted them greatly. It was the hour for the departure of the mails and diligences.

Almost all the stagecoaches to the south and west, passed at that time by the Champs-Elysées. The greater part followed the quai and went out through the Barrière Passy. Every minute some huge vehicle, painted yellow and black, heavily loaded, noisily harnessed, distorted with mails, awnings, and valises, full of heads that were constantly disappearing, grinding the curbstones, turning the pavements into flints, rushed through the crowd, throwing out sparks like a forge, with

dust for smoke, and an air of fury. This hubbub delighted the young girls. Favourite exclaimed:

"What an uproar; one would say that heaps of chains were taking flight."

It so happened that one of these vehicles which could be distinguished with difficulty through the obscurity of the elms, stopped for a moment, then set out again on a gallop. This surprised Fantine.

"It is strange," said she. "I thought the diligences never stopped."

Favourite shrugged her shoulders:

"This Fantine is surprising; I look at her with curiosity. She wonders at the most simple things. Suppose that I am a traveller, and say to the diligence; 'I am going on; you can take me up on the quai in passing.' The diligence passes, sees me, stops and takes me up. This happens every day. You know nothing of life, my dear."

Some time passed in this manner.

Suddenly Favourite started as if from sleep.

"Well!" said she, "and the surprise?"

"Yes," returned Dahlia, "the famous surprise."

"They are very long!" said Fantine.

As Fantine finished the sigh, the boy who had waited at dinner entered. He had in his hand something that looked like a letter.

"What is that?" asked Favourite.

"It is a paper that the gentlemen left for these ladies," he replied.

"Why did you not bring it at once?"

"Because the gentlemen ordered me not to give it to the ladies before an hour," returned the boy.

Favourite snatched the paper from his hands. It was really a letter.

"Stop!" said she. "There is no address; but see what is written on it:

"THIS IS THE SURPRISE."

She hastily unsealed the letter, opened it, and read (she knew how to read):

"Oh, our lovers!

"Know that we have parents. Parents—you scarcely know the meaning of the word, they are what are called fathers and mothers in the civil code, simple but honest. Now these parents bemoan us, these old men claim us, these good men and women call us prodigal sons, desire our return and offer to kill for us the fatted calf. We obey them, being virtuous. At the moment when you read this, five met-

tlesome horses will be bearing us back to our papas and mammas. We are pitching our camps, as Bossuet says. We are going, we are gone. We fly in the arms of Lafitte, and on the wings of Caillard. The Toulouse diligence snatches us from the abyss, and you are this abyss, our beautiful darlings! We are returning to society, to duty and order, on a full trot, at the rate of three leagues an hour. It is necessary to the country that we become, like everybody else, prefects, fathers of families, rural guards, and councillors of state. Venerate us. We sacrifice ourselves. Mourn for us rapidly, and replace us speedily. If this letter rends you, rend it in turn. Adieu.

"For nearly two years we have made you happy. Bear us no ill will for it."

"*Signed:* BLACHEVILLE,
　　　FAMEUIL,
　　　LISTOLIER,
　　　FELIX THOLOMYÈS
"P.S. The dinner is paid for."

The four girls gazed at each other.

Favourite was the first to break silence.

"Well!" said she, "it is a good farce all the same."

"It is very droll," said Zéphine.

"It must have been Blacheville that had the idea," resumed Favourite. "This makes me in love with him. Soon loved, soon gone. That is the story."

"No," said Dahlia, "it is an idea of Tholomyès. This is clear."

"In that case," returned Favourite, "down with Blacheville, and long live Tholomyès!"

"Long live Tholomyès!" cried Dahlia and Zéphine.

And they burst into laughter.

Fantine laughed like the rest.

An hour afterwards, when she had re-entered her chamber, she wept. It was her first love, as we have said; she had given herself to this Tholomyès as to a husband, and the poor girl had a child.

LA BOHÈME

An Opera in Four Acts

ACT I SYNOPSIS

Rudolph and Marcel are sitting in the latter's attic-studio in the Quartier Latin, in Paris. Marcel is absorbed in his painting. The day is cold. They have no money to buy coal. Marcel takes a chair to burn it, when Rudolph remembers that he has a manuscript which has been rejected by the publishers and lights a fire with that instead. Colline enters, looking abject and miserable. He had gone out to pawn his books, but nobody wanted them. Their friend, Schaunard, however, had better luck. He comes bringing fuel and provisions. They all prepare their meal, when the landlord enters and demands the payment of his rent. The friends offer him a glass of wine and turn him out amidst joking and laughter. After their gay repast they separate and Rudolph remains alone writing.

A knock is heard at the door and Mimi, a little seamstress, who lives on the same floor, appears and asks Rudolph to give her a match to light her candle. As she is about to go out, she falls in a faint. Rudolph gives her wine and restores her to consciousness. She tells him that she suffers from consumption. Rudolph is struck by her beauty and her delicate hands. She notices that she has lost her key and whilst they search for it their candles are extinguished. As they grope on the floor in the dark, Rudolph finds the key and puts it in his pocket. Their hands meet and Rudolph tries to warm her hands and tells her all about his life. Mimi confides her struggles to him and their conversation soon turns upon their love for each other.

ARRONDISSEMENT 6ÈME

The sixth arrondissement runs from the student-oriented shopping thoroughfare Boulevard Saint Michel, along the charming rue Saint André des Arts, past the Saint Germain des Prés quarter, through the ultra *à la Française* Jardin du Luxembourg, to a chic residential area toward the west. Famous landmarks in this neighborhood are geared more toward eating and drinking than sightseeing—although sitting all afternoon with one coffee (or their famous hot chocolate) on the terrace of the famed café Les Deux Magots (named for a pair of Chinese figurines) is one of the best kinds of sightseeing Paris offers. Its archrival Café de Flore is next door, and Brasserie Lipp is across the street. Although these cafés were once favored meeting places of artists and philosophers, Picasso and Sartre have largely been replaced by Joe Tourist.

It may seem tempting, but don't even think about playing on the grass at the Jardin du Luxembourg, the French Senate's garden, which now occupies Catherine de Médicis' Italianate palace. It is a favorite hangout of Parisians, offering pony rides and puppet shows for the toddler set, toy sailboats for the young at heart, and plenty of shade and benches for the old and tired. Don't miss the gorgeous Fountaine de Médicis, and be sure to watch grizzled old men tangle over whose ball is closest in vicious pétanque matches.

d de la Seine   C. L. C.

Hemingway was one of the most famous American expatriates to live in Paris. Born and raised in Oak Park, Illinois, which he described as "wide lawns and narrow minds," he began working after high school as a cub reporter on the *Kansas City Star*. After six months he left, but kept their style guide (use short sentences, vigorous English, and short first paragraphs) in mind throughout his writing career.

"Papa"
Ernest Hemingway
(1899–1961)

A great outdoorsman and adventurer, he attempted to join the army to get close to the action of World War I. Failing the physical, he signed on with the Red Cross Ambulance Corps instead and first set eyes on Paris (a Paris under bombardment) on his way to the Italian front, where he understandably took up drinking, one of his better-known pastimes.

He next saw Paris as a foreign correspondent for the *Toronto Star*, arriving with his first wife, Hadley, and a letter of introduction to Gertrude Stein. He then proceeded to live what has become a clichéd artist's life: Starving writer revels in the joys of Paris before making it big after writing a best seller (*The Sun Also Rises*) in six weeks while sitting at his favorite café, La Closerie des Lilas.

1n 1928 he left Paris with his second wife, Pauline, for Key West, Florida, and eventually won both the Pulitzer Prize (for *Old Man and the Sea*) and the Nobel Prize in Literature (1954). He died of self-inflicted gunshot wound at his home in Ketchum, Idaho, in 1961.

Other American literary figures of note who stopped awhile in Paris:
James Baldwin, Sylvia Beach, F. Scott Fitzgerald, Janet Flanner, Langston Hughes,
Henry Miller, Ezra Pound, Gertrude Stein, Edmund White.

Right: La Closerie des Lilas by Jean-Pierre Lagrue.

SHAKESPEARE & COMPANY

from A Moveable Feast

by Ernest Hemingway

In those days there was no money to buy books. I borrowed books from the rental library of Shakespeare and Company, which was the library and bookstore of Sylvia Beach at 12 rue de l'Odéon. On a cold windswept street, this was a warm, cheerful place with a big stove in winter, tables and shelves of books, new books in the window, and photographs on the wall of famous writers both dead and living. The photographs all looked like snapshots and even the dead writers looked as though they had really been alive. Sylvia had a lively, sharply sculptured face, brown eyes that were as alive as a small animal's and as gay as a young girl's, and wavy brown hair that was brushed back from her fine forehead and cut thick below her ears

and at the line of the collar of the brown velvet jacket she wore. She had pretty legs and she was kind, cheerful and interested, and loved to make jokes and gossip. No one that I ever knew was nicer to me.

I was very shy when I first went into the bookshop and I did not have enough money on me to join the rental library. She told me I could pay the deposit any time I had the money and made me out a card and said I could take as many books as I wished.

There was no reason for her to trust me. She did not know me and the address I had given her, 74 rue Cardinal Lemoine, could not have been a poorer one. But she was delightful and charming and welcoming and behind her, as high as the wall and stretching out into the back room which gave onto the inner court of the building, were shelves and shelves of the wealth of the library.

I started with Turgenev and took the two volumes of *A Sportsman's Sketches* and an early book of D. H. Lawrence, I think it was *Sons and Lovers,* and Sylvia told me to take more books if I wanted. I chose the Constance Garnett edition of *War and Peace*, and *The Gambler and Other Stories* by Dostoyevsky.

"You won't be back very soon if you read all that," Sylvia said.

"I'll be back to pay," I said. "I have some money in the flat."

"I didn't mean that," she said. "You pay whenever it's convenient."

"When does Joyce come in?" I asked.

"If he comes in, it's usually very late in the afternoon," she said. "Haven't you ever seen him?"

"We've seen him at Michaud's eating with his family," I said. "But it's not

polite to look at people when they are eating, and Michaud's is expensive."

"Do you eat at home?"

"Mostly now," I said. "We have a good cook."

"There aren't any restaurants in your immediate quarter, are there?"

"No. How did you know?"

"Larbaud lived there," she said. "He liked it very much except for that."

"The nearest good cheap place to eat is over by the Panthéon."

"I don't know that quarter. We eat at home. You and your wife must come sometime."

"Wait until you see if I pay you," I said. "But thank you very much."

"Don't read too fast," she said.

Home in the rue Cardinal Lemoine was a two-room flat that had no hot water and no inside toilet facilities except an antiseptic container, not uncomfortable to anyone who was used to a Michigan outhouse. With a fine view and a good mattress and springs for a comfortable bed on the floor, and pictures we liked on the walls, it was a cheerful, gay flat. When I got there with the books I told my wife about the wonderful place I had found.

"But Tatie, you must go by this afternoon and pay," she said.

"Sure I will," I said. "We'll both go. And then we'll walk down by the river and along the quais."

"Let's walk down the rue de Seine and look in all the galleries and in the windows of the shops."

"Sure. We can walk anywhere and we can stop at some new café where we don't know anyone and nobody knows us and have a drink."

"We can have two drinks."

"Then we can eat somewhere."

"No. Don't forget we have to pay the library."

"We'll come home and eat here and we'll have a lovely meal and drink Beaune from the co-operative you can see right out of the window there with the price of the Beaune on the window.

And afterwards we'll read and then go to bed and make love."

"And we'll never love anyone else but each other."

"No. Never."

"What a lovely afternoon and evening. Now we'd better have lunch."

"I'm very hungry," I said. "I worked at the café on a café crème."

"How did it go, Tatie?"

"I think all right. I hope so. What do we have for lunch?"

"Little radishes, and good *foie de veau* with mashed potatoes and an endive salad. Apple tart."

"And we're going to have all the books in the world to read and when we go on trips we can take them."

"Would that be honest?"

"Sure."

"My," she said. "We're lucky that you found the place."

"We're always lucky," I said and like a fool I did not knock on wood. There was wood everywhere in that apartment to knock on too.

Le Cocktail

Aperitifs
(before dinner)

KIR. Dry white wine with crème de cassis (blackcurrant liqueur).

KIR ROYAL. Same as Kir, but with champagne instead of white wine.

COMMUNARD or CARDINALE. Red wine with crème de cassis.

LILLET. A red or white wine typically served over ice with or without soda.

CHAMPAGNE. *Une coupe de champagne* is a classic.

SIROPS À L'EAU. Brightly colored drinks. Green: Mint syrup and water. Red: Grenadine and water.

À LA MODE (current fad). Mojito, Piña Colada, Ti'Punch, Sangria, Gin Fiz.

Wine

The house wine in Paris is almost always quite good, or at least not bad. *Un verre* is a glass. *Quart* is 250 ml (about one and a half glasses). *Demi* is 500 ml (about three glasses). A *pichet* is a pitcher of house wine you can order in 250, 500, or 750 ml. A *bouteille* is a full bottle (750 ml).

Looking for a good buy on wine? Try any supermarket or the chain store Nicolas.

Beer

Une pression is from the tap.

Un demi is a normal glass of tap beer.

Digestifs
(after dinner)

Cognac (brandy), Armagnac (brandy), and Calvados (apple brandy).

ARRONDISSEMENT 7ÈME

Although this neighborhood is overflowing with tourist blockbusters, it can also be surprisingly quiet and residential. While the natives walk their dogs on the Champ de Mars or along the Seine, out-of-towners visit the Eiffel Tower, the Musée d'Orsay, Musée du Quai Branly, and Les Invalides (originally a hospital and an old age home for veterans that now contains the army museum and Napoleon's tomb).

Neighborhood residents include the prime minister, whose official residence is the Hôtel Matignon, and many government buildings including the headquarters of UNESCO (the United Nations Educational, Scientific and Cultural Organization), where you can meditate among the cherry trees and bamboo in Isamu Noguchi's Japanese garden. The Assemblée Nationale (Parliament's lower house, which was formerly the Bourbon palace) is also located here.

For shopping historians Bon Marché (which misleadingly translates as "bargain") on rue de Sèvres is considered the first department store, and it is deluxe. Gustave Eiffel's metalworking skills were employed during the store's 1868 expansion.

Two of the most unusual museums in town are located in the seventh: the Musée Rodin (Rodin's work is housed in a lovely 18th-century house with a spectacular garden) and Musée des Égouts de Paris (the not-so-lovely sewers-of-Paris museum).

Cheese lovers should skip the sewers and proceed directly to Fromagerie Cantin (12 rue du Champ de Mars), where the Cantin family has been selling France's best Camembert, Brie, Gruyère, and even Beaufort for over half a century. Their selection and expertise will astound you.

MY LIFE IN FRANCE

by Julia Child

Surrounded by gorgeous food, wonderful restaurants, and a kitchen at home—and an appreciative audience in my husband—I began to cook more and more. In the late afternoon, I would wander along the quay from the Chambre des Députés to Notre Dame, poking my nose into shops and asking the merchants about everything. I'd bring home oysters and bottles of Montlouis-Perle de la Touraine, and would then repair to my third-floor *cuisine*, where I'd whistle over the stove and try my hand at ambitious recipes, such as veal with turnips in a special sauce.

But I had so much more to learn, not only about cooking, but about shopping and eating and all the many new (to me) foods. I hungered for more information.

It came, at first, from Hélène, my local guide and language coach. She was a rather knowing instructor, and soon I began to use her French slang and to see Paris as she saw it. Although she wasn't very interested in cooking, Hélène loved to eat and knew a lot about restaurants. One day she loaned me a great big old-fashioned cookbook by the famed chef Ali-Bab. It was a real *book:* the size of an unabridged dictionary, printed on thick paper, it must have weighed eight pounds. It was written in old French, and was out of print, but was full of the most succulent recipes I'd ever seen. And it was also very amusingly written, with little asides about cooking in foreign lands and an appendix on why gourmets are fat. Even on sunny days, I'd retreat to my bed and read Ali-Bab—"with the passionate devotion of a fourteen-year-old boy to *True Detective* stories," Paul noted, accurately.

I had worked on my French diligently, and was able to read better and say a little more every day. At first my communications in the marketplace had consisted of little more than finger-pointing and simplistic grunts: *"Bon! Ça! Bon!"* Now when I went to L'Olivier, the olive-oilery on the Rue de Rivoli—a small shop filled with crocks of olives and bottles of olive oil—I could actually carry on a lengthy conversation with the jolly olive man.

My tastes were growing bolder, too. Take snails, for instance. I had never thought of eating a *snail* before, but, my, tender escargots bobbing in garlicky butter were one of my happiest discoveries! And truffles, which came in a can, and were so deliciously musky and redolent of the earth, quickly became an obsession.

I shopped at our neighborhood marketplace on la Rue de Bourgogne, just around the corner from 81. My favorite person there was the vegetable woman, who was known as Marie des Quatre Saisons because her cart was always filled with the freshest produce of each season. Marie was a darling old creature, round and vigorous, with a crease-lined face and expressive, twinkling eyes. She knew everyone and everything, and she quickly sized me up as a willing disciple. I bought mushrooms or turnips or zucchini from her several times a week; she taught me all about shallots, and how to tell a good potato from a bad one. She took great pleasure in instructing me about which vegetables were best to eat, and when; and how to prepare them correctly. In the meantime, she'd fill me in on so-and-so's wartime experience, or where to get a watchband fixed, or what the weather would be tomorrow. These informal conversations helped my

French immeasurably, and also gave me the sense that I was part of a community.

We had an excellent *crémerie*, located on the *place* that led into the Rue de Bourgogne. It was a small and narrow store, with room for just five or six customers to stand in, single-file. It was so popular that the line would often extend out into the street. Madame la Proprietress was robust, with rosy cheeks and thick blond hair piled high, and she presided from behind the counter with cheerful efficiency. On the wide wooden shelf behind her stood a great mound of freshly churned, sweet, pale-yellow butter waiting for pieces to be carved as ordered. Next to the mound sat a big container of fresh milk, ready to be ladled out. On the side counters stood the cheese—boxes of Camembert, large hunks of Cantal, and wheels of Brie in various stages of ripeness— some brand-new and almost hard,

others soft to the point of oozing.

The drill was to wait patiently in line until it was your turn, and then give your order clearly and succinctly. Madame was a whiz at judging the ripeness of cheese. If you asked for a Camembert, she would cock an eyebrow and ask at what time you wished to serve it: would you be eating it for lunch today, or at dinner tonight, or would you be enjoying it a few days hence? Once you had answered, she'd open several boxes, press each cheese intently with her thumbs, take a big sniff, and—*voilà!*—she'd hand you just the right one. I marveled at her ability to calibrate a cheese's readiness down to the hour, and would even order cheese when I didn't need it just to watch her in action. I never knew her to be wrong.

The neighborhood shopped there, and I got to know all the regulars. One of them was a properly dressed maid who shopped in the company of her

household's proud, prancing black poodle. I saw her on a regular basis, and she was always dressed in formless gray or brown clothes. But one day I noticed that she had arrived without the poodle and dressed in a new, trim black costume. I could see the eyes of everyone in line shifting to observe her. As soon as Madame spotted the new finery, she summoned the maid to the front of the line and served her with great politesse. When she swept by me and out the door with a slight Mona Lisa smile on her lips, I asked my neighbor in line why the maid had been given such deferential treatment.

"She has a new job," the woman explained, with a knowing look. "She works for *la comtesse*. Did you see how she's dressed today? Now she's practically a *comtesse* herself!"

I laughed, and as I approached Madame to give my order, I thought: "So much for the French Revolution."

. . .

August in Paris was known as *la morte-saison,* "the dead season," because everybody who could possibly vacate did so as quickly as possible. A great emptying out of the city took place, as hordes migrated toward the mountains and coasts, with attendant traffic jams and accidents. Our favorite restaurants, the creamery, the meat man, the flower lady, the newspaper lady, and the cleaners all disappeared for three weeks. One afternoon I went into Nicolas, the wine shop, to buy some wine and discovered that everyone but the deliveryman had left town. He was minding the store, and in the meantime was studying voice in the hope of landing a role at the opera. Sitting next to him was an old concierge who, twenty-five years earlier, had been a seamstress for one of the great couturiers on la Place Vendôme. She and the deliveryman reminisced about the golden days of Racine and Molière and the Opéra

Comique. I was delighted to stumble in on these two. It seemed that in Paris you could discuss classic literature or architecture or great music with everyone from the garbage collector to the mayor.

On August 15, I turned thirty-seven years old. Paul bought me the *Larousse Gastronomique,* a wonder-book of 1,087 pages of sheer cookery and foodery, with thousands of drawings, sixteen color plates, all sorts of definitions, recipes, information, stories, and gastronomical know-how. I devoured its pages even faster and more furiously than I had Ali-Bab.

By now I knew that French food was *it* for me. I couldn't get over how absolutely delicious it was. Yet my friends, both French and American, considered me some kind of a nut: cooking was far from being a middle-class hobby, and they did not understand how I could possibly enjoy doing all the shopping and cooking and serv-ing by myself. Well, I did! And Paul encouraged me to ignore them and pursue my passion.

I had been cooking in earnest at Roo de Loo, but something was missing. It was no longer enough for me to salivate over recipes in the *Larousse Gastronomique,* or chat with Marie des Quatre Saisons, or sample my way through the menus of wonderful restaurants. I wanted to roll up my sleeves and dive into French cuisine. But how?

Out of curiosity, I dropped by L'École du Cordon Bleu, Paris's famous cooking school. There professional chefs taught traditional French cooking to serious students from all over the world. After attending a demonstration one afternoon, I was hooked.

The next class began in October. I signed myself up for a six-week intensive course, and smacked my lips in anticipation of the great day.

BŒUF A LA MO

Restaurants, Brasseries & Bistros, Oh My! (The Basics)

Dining, of course, is one of the best things to do in Paris. Personally—if I were forced to choose—I'd skip the Louvre for a meal of cassoulet or magret de canard and a hearty red wine most any day. There are many great restaurants in Paris—so here are some tips to help narrow the search. Every Wednesday the newspaper *Le Figaro,* available at kiosks, has a supplement called "Figaro Scope" with good dining (and entertainment) ideas (figaroscope.fr). The *Zagat Guide* (zagat.com)—where those who nosh get to vote—is the ultimate in democratic dining, while the *Michelin Guide Paris* (red for restaurants and hotels) employs secret inspectors to seek out and test the best restaurants (and hotels) in Paris (nice work if you can get it).

Lunch is between noon and 2 PM, dinner, not before 8:30 PM. Many restaurants are closed Monday and sometimes Sunday too. Make a reservation—especially on weekends. Fifteen percent service is always included (it's the law!), but it's customary to leave 5 to 10 percent more in appreciation of great service. Don't be surprised to see a shih tzu or Yorkie sitting on Madam's lap, even in the best restaurants.

RESTAURANT. Just for dining, not for drinks, and mostly in a (more or less) formal style.

BISTRO (from the Russian word *bistro,* meaning "fast"). Originally managed by wine-merchants-turned-restaurateurs, so a step above a café since they tend to offer a good wine list. Here you'll find simple traditional dishes, reasonable prices, and a *plat du jour* (daily special).

BRASSERIE. These eating establishments (originally breweries) arrived in Paris along with refugees fleeing from war-torn Alsace-Lorraine in 1870, thus their original fare of sauerkraut and beer. Similar to restaurants or bistros, they have a brewery-like decor (think wood and copper) and serve traditional dishes such as onion soup and coq au vin.

LE MENU is the most common way to order—basically a three-course meal at a fixed price with a choice of one starter, one main, and either cheese or dessert.

À LA CARTE. Carte means "menu" in English; à la carte is when you order individual items from the carte, each with its own price.

LA FORMULE is a kind of promotional package mostly used for lunch. You choose either a starter and main or a main and dessert. These run from 13 to 15 euros and are a good buy.

Three 3-Star Michelin Picks

ALAIN DUCASSE AU PLAZA ATHÉNÉE (8è; Métro: Alma Marceau; in the Hôtel Plaza Athénée, 25 ave Montaigne; +33 (0)1 53 67 65 00; contemporary/innovative; Menu, 220–320€). Elegance in a legendary hotel that opened on the prestigious Avenue Montaigne in 1911.

L'AMBROISIE (4è; Métro: Saint Paul; 9 place des Vosges; +33 (0)1 42 78 51 45; reinterpretation of traditional; 185–275€). White tablecloths, antique mirrors, hushed voices in a room located on the beautiful Place des Vosges.

LE MEURICE (1er; Métro: Tuileries; Hôtel le Meurice, 228 rue de Rivoli; +33 (0)1 44 58 10 55; French classics reinvented; Menu, 75 (lunch)/190€). Chef Yannick Alleno chooses only the freshest seasonal foods to create his interpretations of classic French dishes.

Five Top Tables

L'ASTRANCE (16è; Métro: Passy; 4 rue Beethoven; +33 (0)1 40 50 84 40; nouvelle cuisine; Menu, 70 (lunch)/270€) In a small, unstuffy room, the chef improvises from the ingredients at his fingertips to create a brand-new menu daily.

L'ATELIER DE JOËL ROBUCHON (7è; Métro: rue du Bac; 5 rue de Montalembert; +33 (0)1 42 22 56 56; French haute cuisine; Menu, 110€). No reservations are taken at this innovative eatery with red leather stools and a sushi-bar counter specializing in tapas-style tidbits.

LE GRAND VÉFOUR (1er; Métro: Palais Royal–Musée du Louvre; 17 rue de Beaujolais; +33 (0)1 42 96 56 27; French haute cuisine; Menu, 75 (lunch)/250€). Regency decor and inventive twists on tradition are served up at what has been a destination restaurant since 1782.

GUY SAVOY (17è; Métro: Étoile; 18 rue Troyon; +33 (0)1 43 80 40 61; French haute cuisine; Menu, 230–285€). Artichoke soup with black truffles is a favorite at what chef-"innkeeper" Guy Savoy calls "an inn for the 21st century."

PIERRE GAGNAIRE (8è; Métro: Charles de Gaulle–Étoile/George V; 6 rue Balzac; +33 (0)1 58 36 12 50; creative French haute cuisine; Menu, 95 (lunch)/240€). Dynamic cuisine looking

toward tomorrow but with firm roots in the past. There are always surprises on the menu here.

Bourgeois Bargains

BANYAN (15è; Métro: Félix Faure; 24 place E. Pernet; +33 (0)1 40 60 09 31; Thai; 40€). Have a taste of Bangkok in the heart of Paris in this simple but comfortable restaurant; takeout is another option.

LE BISTROT PAUL BERT (11è; Métro: Faidherbe-Chaligny; 18 rue Paul Bert; +33 (0)1 43 72 24 01; old-fashioned bistro; 40€). As bistros go, this is one of the best, from the steak frites to the shellfish.

LE RÉMINET (5è; Métro: Maubert-Mutualité/Saint Michel; 3 rue Grands Degrés; +33 (0)1 44 07 04 24; nouvelle; 50€). A great bistro for lunch after climbing the tower at nearby Notre Dame. They have a rich *cave* giving you plenty of wine choices.

TEMPS AU TEMPS (11è; Métro: Faidherbe-Chaligny; 3 rue Paul Bert; +33 (0)1 43 79 63 40; bistro; Menu, 30€). An adorable, intimate restaurant with simple food well done, all at a great price.

LE TROQUET (15è; Métro: Sèvres-Lecourbe/Volontaire; rue François Bonvin; +33 (0)1 45 66 89 00; bistro with some Basque; Menu, 28 (lunch)/40€).

Down a tiny street in the 15th you'll find some big flavors and reasonable prices; the menu changes daily.

Just Desserts

BERTHILLON (4è; Métro: Pont Marie; 31 rue Saint Louis en l'Île; +33 (0)1 43 54 31 61; ice cream is the specialty; 5€). All-natural ingredients make up some of the best ice cream in the city; ginger caramel, coffee-whiskey, chestnut, and Earl Grey are just some of their *parfums*.

JEAN-PAUL HÉVIN (1er; Métro: Madeleine/Tuileries; 231 rue Saint Honoré; +33 (0)1 55 35 35 96; 6€). One of the most famous chocolatiers in Paris offers an extensive pastry menu in its tearoom; tartelette au chocolat, sablé cassis, and hot chocolate should not be missed.

LADURÉE (6è; Métro: Saint Sulpice; 21 rue Bonaparte; +33 (0)1 44 07 64 87; 5€). They sell over 375 kg of their famous macaroons daily at this traditional, handsome patisserie/tea salon that's been around since 1862.

LA TABLE D'HÉDIARD (8è; Métro: Madeleine; 21 place Madeleine; +33 (0)1 43 12 88 99; 7€). Shop for luxury gifts in the gourmet shop then stop for a snack in the tearoom 3–6 PM.

La Tour Eiffel

"this truly tragic street lamp"

"this belfry skeleton"

*"this high and skinny
pyramid of iron ladders . . .
which just peters out into
a ridiculous thin shape like
a factory chimney"*

*"a carcass waiting to be
fleshed out with freestone or
brick, a funnel-shaped grill,
a hole-riddled suppository"*

*"this mast of iron gymnasium
apparatus, incomplete, confused and deformed"*

*"its barbarous mass over-
whelming and humiliating all
our monuments . . . for twenty
years we shall see spreading
across the whole city, a city
shimmering with the genius of
so many centuries, we shall see
spreading like an ink stain, the
odious shadow of this odious
column of bolted metal"*

These are just some of the comments published in 1887 as construction began on Gustav Eiffel's masterpiece, designed as the entrance for the Universal Exposition of 1889. Fortunately for Paris, the tower had been rejected for the 1888 exposition in Barcelona. But even those who chose the design weren't all that confident. The contest rules called for a structure that could be easily deconstructed, and in fact Eiffel's contract called for the removal of the tower in 1909. But luckily for the rest of the world, by then it was being used as an important communications tower (radio and eventually TV) and was allowed to stay. Whatever your opinion of its beauty, it remains the most visited monument on the planet.

ARRONDISSEMENT 8ÈME

The triangle made up of the Champs-Élysées, Avenue Montaigne, and Avenue George V is known as le Triangle d'Or (golden triangle). Although the Champs-Élysées tends toward the pedestrian—tourists speaking every imaginable language schlepping along in their shorts and flip-flops slurping ice cream cones—around the corner the very short, very fashionable Avenue Montaigne is pure deluxe. Louis Vuitton, Dolce & Gabbana, Ferragamo, Jimmy Choo, Dior, Chanel, Bulgari, and the Plaza Athenée hotel scream opulence—all in 615 short meters.

A bit to the east is the iron-and-glass Grand Palais, an amazing space showing contemporary art. Its little brother, the Beaux-Arts Petit Palais, is across the street. At the eastern end of the Champs-Élysées is the Place de la Concorde, a vast square of never-ending traffic circling the Obelisk of Luxor and two impressive fountains. This—the largest square in Paris—was originally called Place Louis XV, but during the revolution became Place de la Révolution. It is where heads (Louis XVI, Marie Antoinette, and thousands of others) literally rolled.

Just to the north is La Madeleine, an ancient-Roman-temple-ish church dedicated to Mary Magdalene that plays host to some of Paris's most fashionable weddings.

North of the Champs-Élysées is very residential. The president of the republic lives at the Élysée Palace, and Parisians play in the Parc Monceau, one of the most beautiful and well-used parks in Paris.

For classic escargots and crème brûlée (flaming!), drop by Le Boeuf Sur le Toit (34 rue du Colisée), former hangout of Jean Cocteau, and sink into another era at the consummate art deco brasserie.

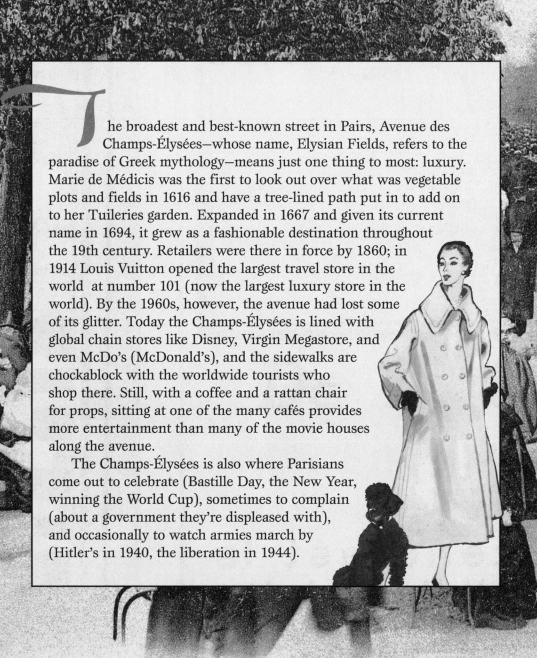

The broadest and best-known street in Pairs, Avenue des Champs-Élysées—whose name, Elysian Fields, refers to the paradise of Greek mythology—means just one thing to most: luxury. Marie de Médicis was the first to look out over what was vegetable plots and fields in 1616 and have a tree-lined path put in to add on to her Tuileries garden. Expanded in 1667 and given its current name in 1694, it grew as a fashionable destination throughout the 19th century. Retailers were there in force by 1860; in 1914 Louis Vuitton opened the largest travel store in the world at number 101 (now the largest luxury store in the world). By the 1960s, however, the avenue had lost some of its glitter. Today the Champs-Élysées is lined with global chain stores like Disney, Virgin Megastore, and even McDo's (McDonald's), and the sidewalks are chockablock with the worldwide tourists who shop there. Still, with a coffee and a rattan chair for props, sitting at one of the many cafés provides more entertainment than many of the movie houses along the avenue.

The Champs-Élysées is also where Parisians come out to celebrate (Bastille Day, the New Year, winning the World Cup), sometimes to complain (about a government they're displeased with), and occasionally to watch armies march by (Hitler's in 1940, the liberation in 1944).

The Champs-Élysées

Les Champs-Élysées

BY MIKE WILSH, MIKE DEIGHAN
AND PIERRE DELANOË

Je m'baladais sur l'avenue le coeur ouvert à l'inconnu

    (I strolled down the avenue, my heart opened to the unknown)

J'avais envie de dire bonjour à n'importe qui

    (I wanted to say hello to everyone)

N'importe qui et ce fut toi, je t'ai dit n'importe quoi

    (Everyone, it could be you, I'd said anything to you)

Il suffisait de te parler, pour t'apprivoiser

    (It was enough to speak to you, just to calm myself)

Aux champs-élysées, aux champs-élysées
    (On the champs-élysées, on the champs-élysées)
Au soleil, sous la pluie, à midi ou à minuit
    (In the sun, in the rain, at noon or midnight)
Il y a tout ce que vous voulez aux champs-élysées
    (There is everything you could want on the champs-élysées)

Tu m'as dit "J'ai rendez-vous dans un sous-sol avec des fous
    (You said to me "I was stuck in the basement with fools)
Qui vivent la guitare à la main, du soir au matin"
    (Who live guitar-in-hand from dusk till dawn")
Alors je t'ai accompagnée, on a chanté, on a dansé
    (Then I followed you, we sang, we danced)

124

et l'on n'a même pas pensé à s'embrasser

    (We did not even think of embracing)

Hier soir deux inconnus et ce matin sur l'avenue

    (Last evening we were two strangers and this

    morning on the avenue)

Deux amoureux tout étourdis par la longue nuit

    (We are two in love, dazed by the long night)

et de l'Étoile à la Concorde, un orchestre à mille cordes

    (And from the Étoile to Concord, there is an orchestra

    with a thousand cords)

Tous les oiseaux du point du jour chantent l'amour

    (All the birds at day-break singing of love)

This Neoclassical church was originally designed to be a temple to celebrate "the glory of the great army" (Napoleon's army, Napoleon's words), but it was not the first house of worship to sit on this site. Back in 1182 there was a synagogue here that was seized by 15-year-old King Philip II (after he banished all Jews from France), which was then "converted" by Bishop Maurice de Sully into a church dedicated to Mary Magdalene.

But between seizure of synagogue and Napoleon's temple, there were many plans for the site. Louis XV wanted a church like that of Les Invalides, but that ended with the architect's death. The next designer started to build a domed church like the Pantheon in Rome, but revolutionaries—who thought a library, ballroom, or market would be more useful—ended that. Even after Napoleon, when Louis XVIII again decided it would be a church dedicated to Saint Mary Magdalene, there was brief talk (in 1837) of using the building as the first train station in Paris.

Boulevard de la Madeleine

BY MIKE PINDER AND DENNY LAINE

She said she'd come, she didn't
I'm the one in love, she isn't
There's no girl standing there
And there's no one who cares
And the trees are so bare
On the Boulevard de la Madeleine

It's a sad day in Paris
With no girl by my side
Got to feeling so badly
Like a part of me died
It would have been
So good to see her
I never thought
She wouldn't be there

Obélisque de Luxor

et on the largest and possibly the most infamous square in Paris is the Obélisque de Luxor, a 230-ton, 33-century-old obelisk of pink granite that was given to France from Mehemet Ali, viceroy of Egypt, in 1831. The square it sits in has so far been called (in this order) Place Louis XV, Place de la Révolution, Place de la Concorde, Place Louis XV (again), Place Louis XVI, Place de la Chartre, and (for the time being) Place de la Concorde (again). But before the obelisk, there was the guillotine—one that saw the removal of nearly 3,000 heads (including Louis XVI's and Marie Antoinette's) between 1793 and 1795.

North of the obelisk is the Hôtel Crillon, where in happier times Marie Antoinette took piano lessons, and where in 1778 France (first in the world) signed a treaty recognizing a free and independent United States of America.

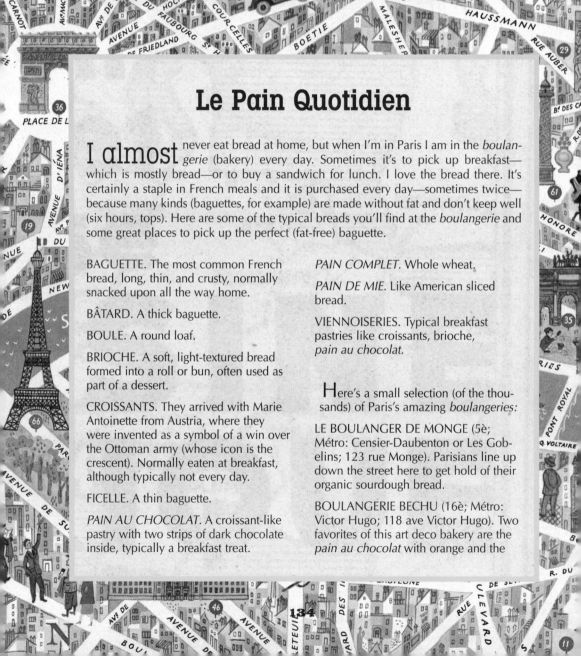

Le Pain Quotidien

I almost never eat bread at home, but when I'm in Paris I am in the *boulangerie* (bakery) every day. Sometimes it's to pick up breakfast—which is mostly bread—or to buy a sandwich for lunch. I love the bread there. It's certainly a staple in French meals and it is purchased every day—sometimes twice—because many kinds (baguettes, for example) are made without fat and don't keep well (six hours, tops). Here are some of the typical breads you'll find at the *boulangerie* and some great places to pick up the perfect (fat-free) baguette.

BAGUETTE. The most common French bread, long, thin, and crusty, normally snacked upon all the way home.

BÂTARD. A thick baguette.

BOULE. A round loaf.

BRIOCHE. A soft, light-textured bread formed into a roll or bun, often used as part of a dessert.

CROISSANTS. They arrived with Marie Antoinette from Austria, where they were invented as a symbol of a win over the Ottoman army (whose icon is the crescent). Normally eaten at breakfast, although typically not every day.

FICELLE. A thin baguette.

PAIN AU CHOCOLAT. A croissant-like pastry with two strips of dark chocolate inside, typically a breakfast treat.

PAIN COMPLET. Whole wheat.

PAIN DE MIE. Like American sliced bread.

VIENNOISERIES. Typical breakfast pastries like croissants, brioche, *pain au chocolat.*

Here's a small selection (of the thousands) of Paris's amazing *boulangeries:*

LE BOULANGER DE MONGE (5è; Métro: Censier-Daubenton or Les Gobelins; 123 rue Monge). Parisians line up down the street here to get hold of their organic sourdough bread.

BOULANGERIE BECHU (16è; Métro: Victor Hugo; 118 ave Victor Hugo). Two favorites of this art deco bakery are the *pain au chocolat* with orange and the

coco-banane, a distinctive coconut banana pastry.

GANACHAUD (20è; Métro: Gambetta; 226 rue des Pyrénées). Fresh breads from wood-burning ovens that many claim are the best in Paris.

GOSSELIN (1er; Métro: Louvre-Rivoli; 125 rue Saint Honoré). Locals rave about their baguette; no wonder it has the honor of being chosen the city's best.

MAISON KAYSER (5è; Métro: Maubert-Mutualité; 14 rue Monge). Although they turn out over 60 different breads daily, they are known for their flaky croissants.

MOULIN DE LA VIERGE (15è; Métro: Ségur or Sèvres-Lecourbe; 166 ave de Suffren). Organic, stone-ground flour and a wood-burning fire are used to make their scrumptious breads.

POILÂNE (6è; Métro: Vaneau or Rennes; 8 rue du Cherche Midi). Seven thousand loaves of their round whole wheat pain Poilâne are made and shipped around Paris and the world every day; this is the only Parisian bread you're likely to find called by the baker's name.

ARRONDISSEMENT 9ÈME

From the Opéra (Palais Garnier) to the Moulin Rouge, the ninth arrondissement is a district of distinct diversions. Originally part of the old village of Montmartre, this butterflyish-shaped neighborhood offers song, shopping, and sex. The Opéra—a spectacular Neo-Baroque confection sometimes referred to as the Palais Garnier to distinguish it from the official opera house at the Bastille—provides entertainment almost daily. Along Boulevard Haussmann, not far from the Opéra, are *les grand magasins*, Printemps and Galeries Lafayette—19th-century department stores that are worth a visit even if you are not shopping. The area around the stores is one of high finance that many banks and insurance companies call home. But a little fun can be had at the nearby Musée Grévin, a campy wax museum/experience.

In the north the bourgeois lifestyle of opera, shopping, and banking gives way to Paris's red-light district, centered along the Boulevard Clichy and Place Pigalle (nicknamed Pig Alley by American GIs after World War II). Here you can find everything from seedy peep shows to the upscale feather-and-rhinestone revues of the Moulin Rouge (technically in the 18th arrondissement). Just down the street (also technically in the 18th arrondissement) is the Musée de L'Érotisme (the Erotic Museum), where peeping is elevated to a fine art.

A bit less explicit is the Musée de la Vie Romantique (Museum of the Romantic Life)—an homage to the Parisian Romantic movement located in the Nouvelle Athènes (new Athens) area.

These days the *branché* (way hip) place to be seen is the odd-ball, faux-bohemian restaurant at the Hôtel Amour (8 rue de Navarin), a (reportedly) rooms-by-the-hour operation—*très cool*.

Place de l'Opéra

This spectacular Neo-Baroque confection designed by Charles Garnier (*right*)—dramatically set smack in the middle of a confluence of crossroads, almost waiting for applause from passersby—was plagued with operatic-style troubles during the 15 years it took to build. There was the subterranean lake beneath it (made famous by Gaston Leroux's novel *Phantom of the Opera*), the Franco-Prussian War, and the collapse of Napoleon's empire, to name a few. Still, velvet was gathered, marble and gold were assembled, cherubs and nymphs were carved, and a marvelous grand staircase was installed by the 1875 inauguration.

On a sweeter note there's Opera Honey: An employee in the props department bought a beehive in 1983 and was keeping it in his apartment until he could bring it to his country home. When that didn't work out he brought the hive to work, put it on the roof, and returned a week later to find the hive overflowing with honey. Opera Honey can be purchased in the opera's gift shop and at nearby luxury food shop Fauchon.

© Patrick GIRAUD

SATORI IN PARIS

by Jack Kerouac

Paris is a place where you can really walk around at night and find what you dont want, O Pascal.

Trying to make my way to the Opera a hundred cars came charging around a blind curve-corner and like all the other pedestrians I waited to let them pass and then they all started across but I waited a few seconds looking the other charging cars over, all coming from six directions—Then I stepped off the curb and a car came around that curve all alone like the chaser running last in a Monaco race and right at me—I stepped back just in time—At the wheel a Frenchman completely convinced that no one else has a right to live or get to his mistress as fast as he does—As a New Yorker I run to dodge the free zipping roaring traffic of Paris but Parisians just stand and then stroll and leave it to the driver— And by God it works, I saw dozens of cars screech to a stop from 70 M.P.H. to let some stroller have his way!

I was going to the Opera also to eat in any restaurant that looked nice, it was one of my sober evenings dedicated to solitary studious walks, but O what grim rainy Gothic buildings and me walking well in the middle of those wide sidewalks so's to avoid dark doorways—What vistas of Nowhere City Night and hats and umbrellas—I couldn't even buy a newspaper— Thousands of people were coming out of some performance somewhere—I went to a crowded restaurant on Boulevard des Italiens and sat way at the end of the bar by myself on a high stool and watched, wet and helpless, as waiters mashed up raw hamburg with Worcestershire sauce and other things and other waiters rushed by holding up steaming trays of good food—The one sympathetic counterman brought menu and Alsatian beer I ordered and I told him to wait awhile—He didnt understand that, drinking without eating at once, because he is partner to the secret of charming French eaters;—they rush at the very beginning with *hors d'oeuvres* and bread, and then plunge into their entrees (this is practically always before even a slug of wine) and then they slow down and start lingering, now the wine to wash the mouth, now comes the *talk,* and now the second half of the meal, wine, dessert and coffee, something I cannae do.

In any case I'm drinking my second beer and reading the menu and notice an American guy is sitting five stools away but he is so mean looking in his absolute disgust with Paris I'm afraid to say "Hey, you American?"—

He's come to Paris expecting he woulda wound up under a cherry tree in blossom in the sun with pretty girls on his lap and people dancing around him, instead he's been wandering the rainy streets alone in all that jargon, doesnt even know where the whore district is, or Notre Dame, or some small cafe they told him about back in Glennon's bar on Third Avenue, *nothing*—When he pays for his sandwich he literally throws the money on the counter "You wouldnt help me figure what the real price is anyway, and besides shove it up your you-know-what I'm going back to my old mine nets in Norfolk and get drunk with Bill Eversole in the bookie joint and all the other things you dumb frogs dont know about," and stalks out in poor misunderstood raincoat and disillusioned rubbers—

Then in come two American schoolteachers of Iowa, sisters on a big trip to Paris, they've apparently got a hotel room round the corner and aint left it except to ride the sightseeing buses which pick em up at the door, but they know this nearest restaurant and have just come down to buy a couple of oranges for tomorrow morning because the only oranges in France are apparently Valencias imported from Spain and too expensive for anything so avid as a quick simple *break* of *fast*. So to my amazement I hear the first clear bell tones of American speech in a week:—"You got some oranges here?"

"*Pardon?*"—the counterman.

"There they are in that glass case," says the other gal.

"Okay—see?" pointing, "two oranges," and showing two fingers, and the counterman takes out the two oranges and puts em in a bag and says crisply thru his throat with those Arabic—Parisian "r's";—

"*Trois francs cinquante.*" In other words, 35¢ an orange but the old gals dont care what it costs and besides they dont understand what he's said.

"What's *that* mean?"

"*Pardon?*"

"Alright, I'll hold out my palm and take your kwok-kowk-kwark out of it, all we want's the oranges" and the two ladies burst into peals of screaming laughter like on the porch and the cat politely removes three francs fifty centimes from her hand, leaving the change, and they walk out lucky they're not alone like that American guy—

I ask my counterman what's real good and he says Alsatian Choucroute which he brings—It's just hotdogs, potatos and sauerkraut, but such hotdogs as chew like butter and have a flavor delicate as the scent of wine, butter and garlic all cooking together and floating out a cafe kitchen door—The sauerkraut no better'n Pennsylvania, potatos we got from Maine to San Jose, but O yes I forgot:—with it all, on top, is a weird soft strip of bacon which is really like ham and is the best bite of all.

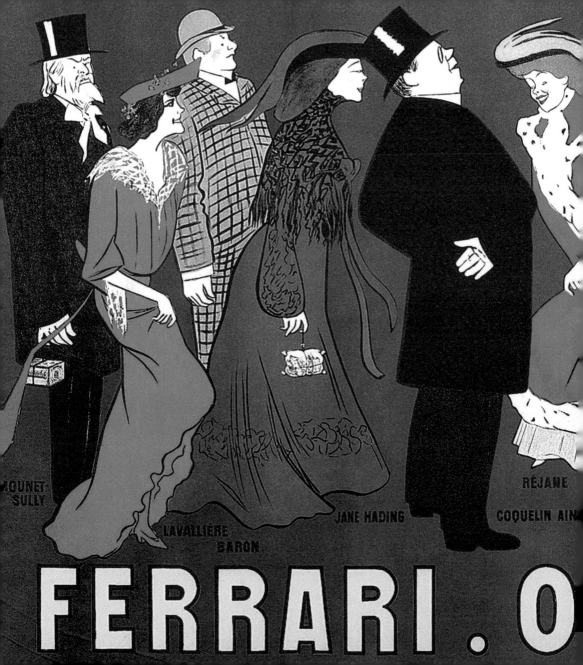

MOUNET-
SULLY

LAVALLIÈRE
BARON.

JANE HADING

RÉJANE

COQUELIN AIN

FERRARI . O

GRANIER

GUITRY

LE BARGY

COQUELIN CADET

BRANDÈS

BRASSEUR

ÉRA . PARIS

I had come to France to do nothing but walk and eat and this was my first meal and my last, ten days.

But in referring back to what I said to Pascal, as I was leaving this restaurant (paid 24 francs, or almost $5 for this simple platter) I heard a howling in the rainy boulevard—A maniacal Algerian had gone mad and was shouting at everyone and everything and was holding something I couldnt see, very small knife or object or pointed ring or something—I had to stop in the door—People hurried by scared—I didn't want to be *seen* by him hurrying away—The waiters came out and watched with me—He approached us stabbing outdoor wicker chairs as he came—The headwaiter and I looked calmly into each other's eyes as tho to say "Are we together?"—But my counterman began talking to the mad Arab, who was actually light haired and probably half French half Algerian, and it became some sort of conversation and

I walked around and went home in a now-driving rain, had to hail a cab.

Romantic raincoats.

. . .

. . . the next afternoon after a good sleep, and me spruced up clean again, I met a Jewish composer or something from New York, with his bride, and somehow they liked me and anyway they were lonely and we had dinner, the which I didnt touch much as I hit up on cognac neat again—"Let's go around the corner and see a movie," he says, which we do after I've talked a half dozen eager French conversations around the restaurant with Parisians, and the movie turns out to be the last few scenes of O'Toole and Burton in "Becket," very good, especially their meeting on the beach on horseback, and we say goodbye—

Again, I go into a restaurant right across from La Gentilhomière recommended to me highly by Jean Tassart, swearing this time I'll have a full course

Paris dinner—I see a quiet man spooning a sumptuous soup in a huge bowl across the way and order it by saying "The same soup as Monsieur." It turns out to be a fish and cheese and red pepper soup as hot as Mexican peppers, terrific and *pink*—With this I have the fresh French bread and gobs of creamery butter but by the time they're ready to bring me the entree chicken roasted and basted with champagne and then sautéed in champagne, and the mashed salmon on the side, the anchovie, the Gruyère, and the little sliced cucumbers and the little tomatos red as cherries and then by God actual fresh cherries for dessert, all *mit* wine of vine, I have to apologize I cant even think of eating anything after all that (my stomach's shrunk by now, lost 15 pounds)—But the quiet soup gentleman moves on to a broiled fish and we actually start chatting across the restaurant and turns out he's the art dealer who sells Arps and Ernsts around the corner,

knows André Breton, and wants me to visit his shop tomorrow. A marvelous man, and Jewish, and we have our conversation in French, and I even tell him that I roll my "r's" on my tongue and not in my throat because I come from Medieval French Quebec-via-Brittany stock, and he agrees, admitting that modern Parisian French, tho dandy, *has* really been changed by the influx of Germans, Jews and Arabs for all these two centuries and not to mention the influence of the fops in the court of Louis Fourteenth which really started it all, and I also remind him that François Villon's real name was pronounced "Ville On" and not "Viyon" (which is a corruption) and that in those days you said not "toi" or "moi" but like "twé" or "mwé" (as we still do in Quebec and in two days I heard it in Brittany) but I finally warned him, concluding my charming lecture across the restaurant as people listened half amused and half attentive, François' name *was* pronounced François and not Françwé for the simple reason that he spelled it Françoy, like the King is spelled Roy, and this has nothing to do with "oi" and if the King had ever heard it pronounced rouwé (rwé) he would not have invited you to the Versailles dance but given you a *roué* with a hood over his head to deal with your impertinent *cou*, or coup, and couped it right off and recouped you nothing but loss.

Things like that—

Maybe that's when my Satori took place. Or how. The amazing long sincere conversations in French with hundreds of people everywhere, was what I really liked, and did, and it was an accomplishment because they couldnt have replied in detail to my detailed points if they hadnt understood every word I said. Finally I began being so cocky I didn't even bother with Parisian French and let loose blasts and *pataraffes* of *chalivarie* French that had them in stitches because they

still understood, oo there, Professor Sheffer and Professor Cannon (my old French "teachers" in college and prep school who used to laugh at my "accent" but gave me A's.)

But enough of that.

Suffice it to say, when I got back to New York I had more fun talking in Brooklyn accents'n I ever had in me life and especially when I got back down South, whoosh, what a miracle are different languages and what an amazing Tower of Babel this world is. Like, imagine going to Moscow or Tokyo or Prague and listening to all *that*.

That people actually understand what their tongues are babbling. And that eyes do shine to understand, and that responses are made which indicate a soul in all this matter and mess of tongues and teeth, mouths, cities of stone, rain, heat, cold, and the whole wooden mess all the way from Neanderthaler grunts to Martian-probe moans of intelligent scientists, nay, all the way from the Johny Hart ZANG of anteater tongues to the dolorous *"la notte, ch'i' passai con tanta pieta"* of Signore Dante in his understood shroud of robe ascending finally to Heaven in the arms of Beatrice.

Speaking of which I went back to see the gorgeous young blonde in La Gentilhommière and she piteously calls me "Jacques" and I have to explain to her my name is "Jean" and so she sobs her "Jean," grins, and leaves with a handsome young boy and I'm left there hanging on the bar stool pestering everybody with my poor loneliness which goes unnoticed in the crashing busy night, in the smash of the cash register, the racket of washing glasses. I want to tell them that we dont all want to become ants contributing to the social body, but individualists each one counting one by one, but no, try to tell that to the in-and-outers rushing in and out the humming world night as the world turns on one axis. The secret storm has become a public tempest.

But Jean-Pierre Lemaire the Young Breton poet is tending the bar, sad and handsome as none but French youths can be, and very sympathetic with my silly position as a visiting drunkard alone in Paris, shows me a good poem about a hotel room in Brittany by the sea but after that shows me a mean-ingless surrealist-type poem about chicken bones on some girl's tongue ("Take it back to Cocteau!" I feel like yelling in English) but I don't want to hurt him, and he's been nice but's afraid to talk to me because he's on duty and crowds of people are at the outdoor tables waiting for their drinks, young lovers head to head, I'da done better staying home and painting the "Mystical Marriage of St. Catherine" after Girolamo Romanino but I'm so enslaved to yak and tongue, paint bores me, and it takes a lifetime to learn how to paint.

La Chanson

French pop vocals in a style known as La Chanson were popular worldwide in the mid–20th century. Typically the songs were sad or about love, or both, and although the genre lost some appeal toward the 1970s, the chanson tradition continues today with singers like Charlotte Gainsbourg (daughter of Jane Birkin and Serge Gainsbourg), Benjamin Biolay, and Chiara Mastroianni (daughter of Catherine Deneuve and Marcello Mastroianni). The movie *Les Chansons d'Amour,* released in 2007, is a chanson lover's dream. Here are a few of the genre's best-known stars and their *super* hits.

CHARLES AZNAVOUR (b. 1924). One of France's most popular singers, he is also well known worldwide for his soulful interpretations and is often described as "the Frank Sinatra of France." His career began when Edith Piaf heard him sing and took him on the road with her. HITS: "Comme Ils Disent," "The Sound of Your Name" (with Liza Minnelli), "For Me Formidable."

BRIGITTE BARDOT (b. 1934). Known mostly for her movie work in the 1950s and 1960s, and her image as the ultimate sex kitten, Bardot also turned out a few hit tunes. HITS: "Bonnie and Clyde" (with Serge Gainsbourg), "La Madrague," "Contact."

JANE BIRKIN (b. 1946). More actress than singer, her first chanson hit was a duet with Serge Gainsbourg (her second husband) called "Je T'Aime . . . Moi Non Plus," which topped the charts in 1969 despite the fact that it was banned in most of Europe. HITS: "Je T'Aime . . . Mon Non Plus" (with Serge Gainsbourg), "Baby Alone in Babylone," "Ex-Fan des Sixties."

GEORGES BRASSENS (1921–1981). His elegant and articulate lyrics brought him fame, but he is also known as one of France's best postwar poets. HITS: "Les Copains d'Abord," "Chanson pour l'Auvergnat," "La Cane de Jeanne."

JACQUES BREL (1929–1978). Belgian by birth, Brel moved to Paris when he was 23 and is also well known as an actor and director of film. The English-speaking world became aware of him via the off-Broadway revue *Jacques Brel Is Alive and Well and Living in Paris.* HITS: "Ne Me Quitte Pas," "Amsterdam," "Mathilde," "My Death."

DALIDA (1933–1987). Born in Cairo but of Italian origins, Dalida won the Miss Egypt pageant in 1954, left for Paris shortly thereafter to become a movie star and singer, and never looked back. HITS: "Besame Mucho," "Bambino," "Garde-Moi la Dernière Danse."

CATHERINE DENEUVE (b. 1943). One of France's best-known actresses, Deneuve also occasionally sings, most notably (and charmingly) in the 1964 movie musical *Les Parapluies de Cherbourg.*

SERGE GAINSBOURG (1928–1991). The bad boy of French chanson, this sexy (if skinny) singer had more than just hits with Brigitte Bardot and Jane Birkin. HITS: "Bonnie and Clyde" (with Brigitte Bardot), "Je T'Aime . . . Moi Non Plus" (with Jane Birkin), "Je Suis Venu Te Dire Que Je M'En Vais."

YVES MONTAND (1921–1991). Born to peasants in rural Italy, Montand was discovered by Edith Piaf, who took him under her wing, so to speak. He is perhaps best known to American audiences as Marilyn Monroe's costar in the 1960 musical comedy *Let's Make Love.* HITS: "Les Feuilles Mortes," "À Paris," "Battling Joe."

EDITH PIAF (1915–1963). Said to be born under a lamppost on the streets of Belleville, she is perhaps the most famous singer to come out of France. Her mournful voice and style of utter despair are unmistakable, making her the ultimate chanteuse. HITS: "Sous le Ciel de Paris," "La Vie en Rose," "Non, Je Ne Regrette Rien."

The all-girl group Les Parisiennes recorded some classic chansons during the 1960s.

ARRONDISSEMENT 10ÈME

Home to two train stations—Gare de l'Est and Gare du Nord (where the Eurostar will leave you at London's Waterloo Station in two and a half hours)—this is a working-class neighborhood of immigrants. The tradition goes back to the end of the Franco-Prussian War in 1870, when trainloads of refugees left Alsace-Lorraine and made the 10th their home. In his book *L'Assommoir* (a tale of 19th-century working-class Paris) Emile Zola described the area thus: ". . . and the chests were hollow merely from inhaling this air, where even gnats could not live, for lack of food." Still, Jewish refugees arrived from Eastern Europe in the early 20th century (some, unfortunately, were shipped back east from the Gare de l'Est during the Nazi occupation, never to return). Today the population includes many North Africans, Turks, Chinese, and Indians.

The area around the Canal Saint Martin (which was slated to be paved over with an eight-lane highway in the 1960s) is described as up-and-coming. Artists are moving in, quirky cafés are springing up, and even a quirky museum, the Musée de l'Éventail (decorative fans), can be found here.

"For me, the 10th . . . is a neighborhood of poets and locomotives . . . propped up by two railway stations."

—LÉON-PAUL FARGUE
FROM HIS 1939 BOOK
LE PIÉTON DE PARIS

One quirky (but fun) place is the hidden wine bar/restaurant Le Coin de Verre (38 rue Sambre et Meuse). From the street you will see nothing, so ring the bell and let your adventure begin.

No American took Paris by storm quite the way Josephine Baker did—in high heels and a skirt made of 16 loosely strung bananas. She became an overnight sensation after performing the wild and erotic Danse Sauvage at the Théatre des Champs-Élysées in 1925, then continued wowing Parisians with performances at the Folies Bergère—sometimes accompanied by her diamond-collar-wearing pet cheetah (Chiquita), who occasionally leapt from the stage into the orchestra pit.

"La Baker"
Josephine Baker
(1906–1975)

Born Freda Josephine McDonald in St. Louis, Missouri, to a washerwoman and vaudeville drummer, Josephine began her showbiz career early and was on the road performing comic sketches by age 14. Three years later she was a chorus girl on Broadway; shortly thereafter she left for Europe to tour in the musical *La Revue Nègre*.

In Paris she felt free of racial oppression for the first time and was easily accepted in artistic circles that included Picasso, F. Scott Fitzgerald, and Hemingway, who called her "the most sensational woman anyone ever saw."

During World War II she was a spy for the resistance, and in the 1950s and 1960s she supported the US civil rights movement—speaking alongside Martin Luther King.

> "I like Frenchmen very much, because even when they insult you they do it so nicely."

Although she was married anywhere from four to six times (depending on whom you ask), she had no biological children. She did, however, adopt 12 children from various ethnicities, calling her family "the Rainbow Tribe."

When Baker died, 20,000 fans clogged the streets around la Madeleine to pay their last respects.

J'ai Deux Amours (two loves)

BY GÉORGES KOGER AND HENRI VARNA

On dit qu'au delà des mers (They say that across the ocean)

La-bas, sous le ciel clair, (There where the sky is clear)

Il existe une cité (There is a city)

Au séjour enchanté, (That enchants)

et sous les grands arbres noirs, (And beneath the large black trees)

chaque soir, (Each night)

Vers elle s'en va tout mon espoir. (Toward it goes all my hope)

J'AI DEUX AMOURS

J'ai deux amours (I have two loves)

Mon pays et Paris (My country and Paris)

Par eux toujours (by them always)

Mon cœur est ravi (My heart is charmed)

Ma savan' est belle (my country is beautiful)

Mais à quoi bon le nier (But why deny)

Ce qui m'ensorcelle (The one that bewitches me)

C'est Paris, Paris tout entier. (That's Paris, entirely Paris.)

PARIS FRANCE

by Gertrude Stein

But still now it is 1939 and war-time, well it was just beginning and everything was agitating and one day we were with our friends the Daniel-Rops they are our neighbors in the country and he was expecting a call to go to Paris and the telephone rang. He went quickly to answer it, he was away some time and we were all anxious. He came back. We said what is it. He said the quenelles the Mère Mollard was making for us have gone soft.

Quenelles, well quenelles are the special dish of this country made of flour and eggs and shredded fish or chicken and pounded by the hour and then rolled and then hardened in the cold air and then cooked in a sauce and they are good.

We all laughed we regretted the quenelles but it was French of her with a son at the front to be worried about her quenelles.

Cooking like everything else in France is logic and fashion.

The French are right when they claim that French cooking is an art and is part of their culture because it is based on latin Roman cooking and has been influenced by Italy and Spain. The crusades only brought them new material, it did not introduce into France the manner of cooking and very little was changed.

French cooking is traditional, they give up the past with difficulty in fact they never do give it up and when they have had reforms so called in the seventeenth century and in the nineteenth century, they only accepted it when it became really a fashion in Paris, but when they took something from the outside like the Polish baba brought by Stanislas Leczinski, the father-in-law of Louis XV or the Austrian croissant brought by Marie Antoinette, they took it over completely so completely that it became French so completely French that no other nation questions it. By the way the Austrian croissant was hurriedly made at the siege of Vienna in 1683 by the Polish soldiers of Sobieski to replace the bread that was missing and they called it the crescent the emblem of the Turks whom they were fighting.

Catherine de Medici in the sixteenth century brought cooks with her and made desserts fashionable, complicated Italian desserts, before that there had been nothing sweet in France except fruits. It was in 1541 that at a ball she introduced these desserts into Paris.

During the time of Henry the Fourth they went back to simple foods as he called himself the king of Gonesse where the best bread in France was made.

The French did though have ideas that one is apt to think of as American and Oriental, roasted ducks with oranges, and stuffed turkeys with raspberries, they ate the turkeys young, and a salad with nuts and apples in the time of Louis XIV.

Cook books were best sellers in France through the seventeenth century and in the introduction to the Dons de Comus, 1739, it was said that "the modern kitchen is a kind of chemistry," so it is evident that cooking in France always was logic and fashion and tradition, which is French.

The ice-creams that came from Italy were water-ices that were soft but they the French with that basis made a solid ice-cream which afterwards they themselves called Neapolitan, which is their way.

The logic of the French cooking is that they used all their material in as complicated ways as they knew and this was refined by foreign influences which became the fashion until the death of Louis the fourteenth and under the Regency they had a full burst of inspired French completely French cooks and cooking, the regent himself had a set of silver casseroles and he did his cooking with his courtiers and it was said that the silver casseroles were not more valuable than the things he put in them. More than half of the dishes of the present great cooking of France were created by the court, the men and the women, the great mistresses of that period were either very religious or very great cooks and sometimes both, the great men around the court were all interested in cooking.

The dishes created by them were named after them, to be sure frequently it was their cooks who really created them but it was the courtier who got the credit and made them the fashion.

Louis XV made his own coffee, he never allowed any one else to make his coffee.

The thing that was particular about all the dishes of that period was the sauces, these dishes practically all were famous because of their sauces, the cooking of the dish was important but the sauce was its creation. The material for the forcemeat of these dishes was developed enormously at this period.

Another thing they discovered then was the use of yolks of eggs for thickening their sauces instead of bread crumbs, and this as is easily seen revolutionised cooking and sauces. This was a purely French invention.

The Revolution of course stopped cooking and under Napoleon who did not know what he was eating, he rarely expressed a preference but he asked his cook to give him some flat

Where shall I begin with the endless delights
Of this Eden of milliners, monkies and sights
This dear busy place, where there's nothing transacting
But dressing and dinnering, dancing and acting?

—Thomas Moore, from *The Fudge Family in Paris*

sausages, his cook disgusted prepared an elaborate dish of finely chopped ingredients, Napoleon ate it without knowing they were not sausages.

But at that moment to save French cooking, Antonin Careme began cooking and he is the creator of present French cooking, but of course much simplified now because then neither material nor work was of any importance.

He made a juice an essence to use in sauces of beef veal and five turkeys and that only should produce a quart of juice.

Traditional again, he went back to the elaborate set dishes really almost of mediaeval France and the Renaissance, but their flavor was elaborated and refined by all the material for cooking that had come into the country since.

Under Louis-Napoleon the writers and poets became the appreciators and critics of cooking as well as the financiers and the court, so Fumas wrote a cook-book, and this went on until the siege of Paris by the Germans and there in the cellars they cooked as elaborately as they knew how to disguise the queer things they had to eat.

When the restaurants became fashionable in the middle of the seventeenth century anybody who had money enough went and in that way learned how to eat, the restaurants had great cooks and really it was through the restaurants that good cooking and fashion in cooking was always diffused throughout France.

The restaurants continued the tradition of popularising complicated and fine cooking that could hardly be done in a simple kitchen and all this until the beginning of the republic after the siege of Paris when everybody more or less at some time even the smallest of the middle classes would be conscious of the great dishes of the French cooking even if not greatly cooked. But in many places they still did cook greatly as well as make the great dishes and that brings me to the Paris I first knew when the Café Anglais still existed.

At the Café Anglais their pride in French cooking expressed itself in the perfection of simple dishes, a saddle of mutton so perfectly and so delicately roasted that in itself it became peaceful and exciting, a roast chicken at Voisin's of the same perfection, sauces instead of being elaborate in these places became simple and perfect, this was in the beginning of the twentieth century.

At the same time as there existed these restaurants who had turned perfect elaboration into perfect simplicity there were the restaurants for the middle classes whose simplicity was beginning to be rather heavy, and the cooking for the lower classes, where simplicity was beginning to be a little too plain and everybody naturally did still talk about cooking.

The hush that always falls when in a French dining-room or in a French restaurant a new dish is presented no matter how poor how rich how simple or how complicated the dish is did still always come but Paris did a little disappoint the provincials when they came to Paris.

I remember being told by a French woman that she could remember when she was a child and they lived in the provinces, the wonder and the awe when Parisians came and brought with them some food from Paris. Now she said the Parisians buy everything they can in the shape of cake or a dish to take with them to Paris. The provinces were having a higher standard of cooking than the capital.

So cooking was decidedly falling off in that period just before the war, they still talked about it, the hush before the new dish was still there, the provinces still had good food, but Paris food was not delicate and perfect any more. And then there was the war.

After the war there was the Americanisation of France, automobiles which kept them from staying at home, cocktails, the worry of spending money instead of saving it, because spending money is always a worry to French people, if they can save life is interesting, if they spend life is dull, and then the introduction of electric stoves and the necessity of not cooking too long, in short French cooking went out and there were very few houses practically none in Paris where cooking was considered an art.

And then slowly it began again. People would begin to talk about some little town far away where a woman cooked, really cooked and everybody would go there no matter how far away it was, the Club of the Hundred formed itself to encourage cooking, the Club of the Four Hundred went beyond the Club of the Hundred.

There was Madame Bourgeois in a little lost town in the centre of France. She and her husband who had been servants in one of the homes in France that still cared for cooking had inherited a little café in this little town that was not on the road to anywhere not even on a railroad. And she began to cook, nobody came except a few fishermen and the local tradesmen and every day she cooked her best dinner for them and then one day after two years of this, a man from Lyon came by accident, a lawyer, and he was pleased with his dinner and he asked her if she could undertake to cook for a dozen of them who were going to celebrate the legion of honor of one of them and she said yes, and from then on the place

was famous and she always tired as she was cooked with the same perfection.

The cooking was simple the twentieth century seemed to want it simple but it was less delicate and a bit richer than the last of the great Paris restaurants.

And so it was the time for the provinces to give the fashion to Paris.

There was no longer a Paris cuisine, there was regional cooking and Paris had to learn from the provinces instead of the provinces learning from Paris.

Last September 1938 when the war did not come one of our friends in the country here, a great cook and a great gourmet, was mobilised a captain of reserve and he had a whole garrison to organise. And I have a charming photograph of him, snapped by a stray visitor, a Polish journalist, he is looking violently at a soldier and the conversation was this. Will you, said Captain d'Aiguy, make us a good risotto, I cannot, my captain, said the soldier who was a cook in one of the big restaurants in Paris, because I have not the foundation of a sauce. Foundation for a sauce, said the captain pale with fury you have material to cook with, everything you want and you cannot make your sauce you have to have a foundation, what do you mean by a foundation. If you please, said the trembling cook, in Paris we always have a foundation for a sauce and we put that in and then mix the sauce. Yes said Captain d'Aiguy and it tastes like it. Let me teach you French cooking. You have the material and you make your sauce.

Well now the war has commenced again 1939 and the soldiers are all talking about their food, and perhaps when they come back there will be a new outburst of French cooking, it was preparing, the foreign influences after the 1914 war have worn themselves off and now everybody is staying at home again and so naturally they will think about cooking.

Mary Cassatt
(1844–1926)

Born in Allegheny City, Pennsylvania, to a wealthy family, Cassatt traveled to Europe as a young girl and never forgot the art she saw there. After attending the Pennsylvania Academy of Fine Arts, she decided—as a young woman of the 19th century—to continue her studies in Paris, concentrating on the Old Masters in the Louvre. There she made the acquaintance of Edgar Degas, who, disenchanted with the powerful Salon (the official art exhibition of the school of Beaux Arts), invited her to participate in a show he was putting together (later labeled the first impressionist exhibition). She accepted and became the only American to exhibit with the original group of impressionists. Her peers included Claude Monet, Auguste Renoir, and Camille Pissarro (the other "rebels" of the Paris art world).

Portrait of Marry Cassatt (left) at the Louvre by Edgar Degas, 1880.

Mary's paintings were often women and children portrayed in everyday life situations like bathing, drinking tea, or simply arranging their hair. She used strong line with soft palettes and today is known as the only woman impressionist.

> "I admired Manet, Courbet, and Degas. I took leave of conventional art. I began to live."

Never one to follow convention or mince words, she said she "hated conventional art," and yet she didn't care for the upstart kids like Henri Matisse and Pablo Picasso, describing their work as "dreadful paintings."

She lived the rest of her life in France, eventually losing her sight; she didn't paint much after 1914.

Other American artists in Paris: Alexander Calder, Winslow Homer, Man Ray, John Singer Sargent, James Whistler.

ARRONDISSEMENT 11ÈME

Best known for the Place de la Bastille—former home to one of the most famous jails in Western history and now home to the postmodern Opéra Bastille (technically in the 12th)—the 11th, while quite historic, remains less touristic than other neighborhoods.

At the heart of the French Revolution and the *grandes révoltes* of the 19th century, the people of the 11th were often the first to rise up and fight. Even during the Nazi occupation of World War II, some of the biggest names of the resistance, many who gave their lives in the fight for liberation, came from this neighborhood.

Today the 11th is better known for its cafés, bars, and restaurants, and the resurgent nightlife of rue Oberkampf and rue du Faubourg Saint Antoine.

Toulouse-Lautrec found lots of inspiration at the Cirque d'Hiver (a curiously round 19th-century building that houses the circus). Likewise, Richard Avedon took his famous photo *Dovima with the Elephants* here. And the building became somewhat famous as background for the 1956 Burt Lancaster/Tony Curtis film *Trapeze*. Today fashion shows and even Turkish wrestling are on the bill.

More serious culture can be found at the Musée Edith Piaf (appointment only, call ahead: 43 55 52 72), a collection of Piaf souvenirs housed in someone's apartment. Le Café Charbon (109 rue Oberkampf), with its tall ceilings, long zinc bar, and tasty French fare, is a great place to try out the *branché* (trendy) Oberkampf nightlife.

CIRQUE D'HIVER

TOUS LES SOIRS
à 8 heures

CIRQUE D'HIVER

La Vie en Rose

BY ÉDITH PIAF

Des yeux qui font baiser les miens,
(Eyes that make mine lower)
Un rire qui se perd sur la bouche
(A laugh lost on his lips)
Voilà le portrait, sans retouche,
(Here is a candid look)
De l'homme auquel j'appartiens.
(at the man I belong to)

THE FRENCH, RUDE? MAIS NON!

by Joseph Voelker

A French academic I know (he's a Spanish professor) told me the story of a confrontation he witnessed in Paris. A retirement-aged American couple approached a Parisian and asked him where "Noder Daaame" was. The man responded by shrugging his shoulders and making a sound that I'm going to spell "PFFFFFT." Then he walked away.

Now, first of all, "PFFFFFT" is part of the French language. It means "I don't know" or "I don't understand." It is neither rude nor hostile. Children respond to teachers and parents with it. It is utterly unrelated to our "raspberry," which is spelled "PHGFPGHF-PFRRRT." The man made this gesture because he was a prisoner inside the difficult French phonetic system, in which *Noder Daaame* cannot by any stretch of the ear and brain be transformed into *"Nuhtr Dom-uh."*

"Okay," you answer. "He didn't understand and he said, 'I don't know.' But why did he walk away instead of trying to help?"

Well, France has been invaded a lot. Caesar arrived in 52 BC. Then there were a half dozen Germanic and Hungarian migrations, followed by the Vikings, who stayed a century. And let's not forget three modern German invasions within a period of seventy years. Sometimes it is difficult for people whose country has never been invaded and occupied to understand people for whom that is a central fact of their national history. It is not admirable on the part of the French that they are not crazy about foreigners, but it runs very, very deep.

Hence, when the French insist on answering our noble efforts at their language by speaking English, we should be more forgiving. First, these are tired people trying to get through a day's work with dead-end jobs in the tourism industry. Second, they are sparing us from looking ridiculous, and thus embarrassing them in turn.

Early in my own sojourn in France, when I was by no means linguistically up to snuff, I found myself in the express lane of a grocery store. A tall young man challenged me—I didn't catch all the words—for being in the wrong lane. I stammered out an answer, to which he replied, *"Oh, M'sieur, vous ne parlez pas Français"* ("You don't speak French"). Instead of letting it go, I said, *"Mais, essayez-moi"* ("Try me"), unaware that the phrase is a standard homosexual come-on. Only his wife derived any enjoyment from the scene, and her *"Oh, Jean-Pierre, oh la la la la la la!"* will stay with me until I die.

Once I inadvertently told a French family gathered at the dinner table that my mother used to make wonderful jellies and she never put condoms in them (*les préservatifs*). Once I phoned a neighbor to ask directions to a famous château and, wanting to know if she thought it was worth a visit, tried to ask, *"Vous l'avez vu?"* ("Have you seen it?") But the American phonetic system (and my untrained mouth) couldn't distinguish among the different French *u's,* and so what I actually said was *"Vous lavez-vous?"* ("Do you bathe yourself?") She laughed inexplicably. An hour after hanging up, I realized what I'd said.

. . .

Just learning the body language to enter and order something in a bakery in France is a small challenge. Somehow we Americans never know where to stand. We end up dead center in the store, with everyone staring at us. I can offer some advice for negotiating small shops.

Begin with *"Bonjour,"* followed always by *"m'sieur"* or *"madame."* (*"Bonjour"* by itself is rather abrupt—even, well, rude. In fact, I'd bet that that retired American couple approached that Parisian in a manner that seemed awfully brusque by his lights.) When you are handed your bag of croissants, say *"Merci, M'sieur,"* or *"Merci, Madame."* And always say *"Au revoir"* or *"Bonne journée"* or something equivalent when you leave. If that's all the French you ever speak, you'll be thought of as an intriguingly polite American.

La Marseillaise

BY CLAUDE JOSEPH ROUGET DE LISLE

Allons, enfants de la Patrie (Arise, children of our country)

Le jour de gloire est arrivé! (The day of glory has arrived!)

Contre nous de la tyrannie, (Against us, tyranny)

L'étendard sanglant est levé. (Has raised its bloody banner)

Entendez-vous dans les campagnes (Do you hear in the fields)

Mugir ces féroces soldats? (The howling of these savage soldiers?)

Ils viennent jusque dans nos bras, (They are coming into our midst)

Égorger nos fils, nos compagnes!

(To cut the throats of our sons, our wives!)

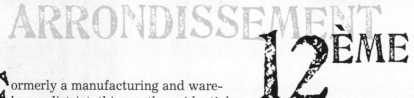

ARRONDISSEMENT 12ÈME

Formerly a manufacturing and warehouse district, this mostly residential neighborhood doesn't offer much for the glamour-seeking tourist to gawk at. Instead the 12th is best understood and explored more as a Parisian might. Take a walk along the Promenade Plantée, a kind of in-the-sky park that runs along the old train viaduct from the Bastille for four kilometers to the Bois de Vincennes. Search below the viaduct for up-and-coming artists or have your violin repaired at the studios built into the arches (le Viaduc des Arts). These studios continue the long tradition of arts and crafts in the 12th. Furniture makers, jewelers, and wood gilders share space with violin makers and fabric designers. Have a drink in Bercy, where wine warehouses have been converted to boutiques and cafés. Shop for fruit and veg at the Marché d'Aligre, a typically Parisian food market, and bring a pitcher or punch bowl to buy your wine because it's sold right from the spigot out of the barrel! Take in basketball, boxing, or an Elton John concert at the Palais Omnisports, an arena located on the river. See an opera at Opéra Bastille, a steel-and-glass theater that opened in 1989 to replace the irreplaceable Palais Garnier. Explore Chinatown around Gare de Lyon, where 140,000 Chinese workers came to help during World War I and stayed to start the first Chinese community in Paris.

Le Fromage

For those who think Brie and Camembert is all there is to French cheese, Paris will be an awakening. There are at least 363 other varieties of French cheese to choose from, enough to try a new kind every day for a year. Cheese is available at the supermarket, but the quality (and service) will be much better at a *fromagerie* (cheese shop), where the cheese is likely to be from a small producer or farmer rather than a factory. They will also give you a taste or two or three and be more than happy to share their extensive expertise. It's not like you can eat any cheese on any day. It might not be in season, it might not be *bien fait* (done), as I found out one day trying to buy a Camembert. The woman behind the counter asked—much to my surprise—when I planned to eat the cheese. She then proceeded to tell me that the particular wheel I wanted could not possibly be eaten before Thursday for lunch and if I wanted to have some cheese sooner, she would choose a different one for me. Here are just a few of the dozens and dozens of *fromageries* found in Paris.

ALAIN DUBOIS (8è; Métro: Péreir; 79 rue de Courcelles). This shop claims to have the largest collection of chèvre (goat cheese) in the capital.

ANDROUET (5è; Métro: Censier Daubenton; 134 rue Mouffetard). This family-run business has been turning out cheeses since 1909. They currently have over 200 in their collection along with a very passionate staff.

BARTHÉLÉMY (7è; Métro: rue du Bac; 51 rue de Grenelle). Roland Barthélémy, cheese master of this tiny shop, offers over 260 varieties. He will put a cheese tray together especially for your soirée.

FROMAGERIE QUATREHOMME (7è; Métro: Vaneau; 62 rue de Sèvres). The farm-made cheeses of Marie Quatrehomme, Maître-fromager (master cheese maker) who was elected Meilleur Ouvrier de France (best craftsman), are popular with the local restaurateurs.

MARIE-ANNE CANTIN (7è; Métro: Ecole Militaire; 12 rue du Champ de Mars). One of the best-known *fromageries* in town. You can join a tasting session chez Marie-Anne and learn the history of cheese along with how to better choose, cut, and save it.

Burgundy makes you think of silly things; Bordeaux makes you talk about them, and Champagne makes you do them.

—Jean Anthelme Brillat-Savarin

Brillat-Savarin is a luscious, triple cream cheese named for Jean Anthelme Brillat-Savarin (1755–1826), perhaps France's most famous gastronome and food writer. It is rich and buttery, and develops a slight sourness as it ripens. Serve it with medjool dates and champagne.

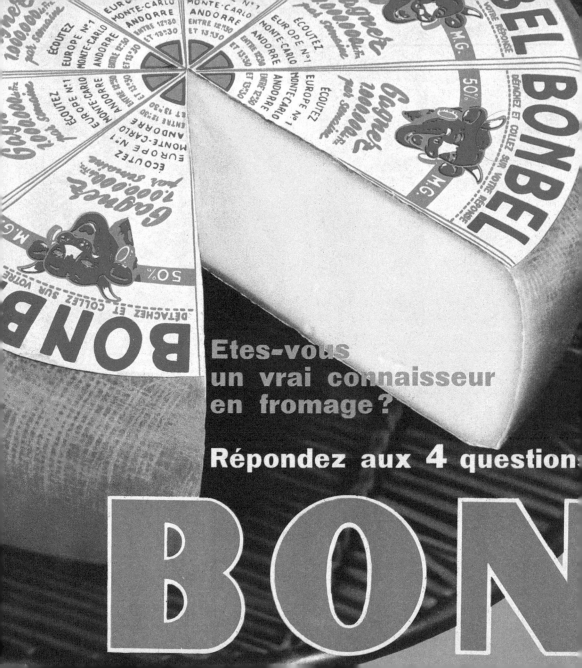

Etes-vous
un vrai connaisseur
en fromage?

Répondez aux 4 question:

ARRONDISSEMENT 13ÈME

So close to the Latin Quarter yet worlds away, this is more the living Paris than the preserved Paris. There are no great museums in the 13th, although the Bibliothèque Nationale de France (the national library) is located here in four towering glass buildings designed to resemble open books, its object: to have one copy of every French book ever published. They have shelf space for 20 million books.

Aside from the library, history and preservation are left to other neighborhoods. The 13th is where Europe's largest Chinatown (*quartier chinois*) along with a thriving Vietnamese community are found among a group of strangely Miami-ish high-rise housing blocks. Two neighborhood shops of note are Paristore and Tang Frères (48 ave d'Ivry), neighboring supermarkets that carry Asian specialties. Cantonese music plays and Buddhists pray at the nearby Temple du Culte de Bouddha (70 avenue d'Ivry).

More charming (practically rural) is the Butte aux Cailles (quail hill), almost a village unto itself; many bars and restaurants are found among its narrow lanes. Bars and discotheques have also popped up on the barges in the Seine adjacent to the neighborhood.

Historically, manufacturing and the decorative arts go a long way back in the 13th. The Manufacture des Goblins (the royal tapestry/furniture/upholstery factory) was opened for Louis XIV in 1662. It survived the revolution (barely) and is still weaving tapestries today for palaces, castles, and state buildings.

At the end of the neighborhood is Orly Airport.

ME TALK PRETTY ONE DAY

by David Sedaris

At the age of forty-one, I am returning to school and have to think of myself as what my French textbook calls "a true debutant." After paying my tuition, I was issued a student ID, which allows me a discounted entry fee at movie theaters, puppet shows, and Festyland, a far-flung amusement park that advertises with billboards picturing a cartoon stegosaurus sitting in a canoe and eating what appears to be a ham sandwich.

I've moved to Paris with hopes of learning the language. My school is an easy ten-minute walk from my apartment, and on the first day of class I arrived early, watching as the returning students greeted one another in the school lobby. Vacations were recount- ed, and questions were raised concern- ing mutual friends with names like Kang and Vlatnya. Regardless of their nationalities, everyone spoke in what sounded to me like excellent French. Some accents were better than others, but the students exhibited an ease and confidence I found intimidating. As an added discomfort, they were all young, attractive, and well dressed, causing me to feel not unlike Pa Kettle trapped backstage after a fashion show.

The first day of class was nerve- racking because I knew I'd be expect- ed to perform. That's the way they do it here—it's everybody into the lan- guage pool, sink or swim. The teacher marched in, deeply tanned from a recent vacation, and proceeded to rattle off a series of administrative announcements. I've spent quite a few summers in Normandy, and I took a monthlong French class before leaving New York. I'm not completely in the dark, yet I understood only half of what this woman was saying.

"If you have not *meimslsxp* or *lgpdmurct* by this time, then you should not be in this room. Has everyone *apzkiubjxow*? Everyone? Good, we shall begin." She spread out her lesson plan and sighed, saying, "All right, then, who knows the alphabet?"

It was startling because (a) I hadn't been asked that question in a while and (b) I realized, while laughing, that I myself did *not* know the alphabet. They're the same letters, but in France they're pronounced differently. I know the shape of the alphabet but had no idea what it actually sounded like.

"Ahh." The teacher went to the board and sketched the letter *a*. "Do we have anyone in the room whose first name commences with an *ahh*?"

Two Polish Annas raised their hands, and the teacher instructed them to present themselves by stating their names, nationalities, occupations, and a brief list of things they liked and disliked in this world. The first Anna hailed from an industrial town outside of Warsaw and had front teeth the size of tombstones. She worked as a seamstress, enjoyed quiet times with friends, and hated the mosquito.

"Oh, really," the teacher said. "How very interesting. I thought that everyone loved the mosquito, but here, in front of all the world, you claim to detest him. How is it that we've been blessed with someone as unique and original as you? Tell us, please."

The seamstress did not understand what was being said but knew that this was an occasion for shame. Her rabbity mouth huffed for breath, and she stared down at her lap as though the appropriate comeback were stitched somewhere alongside the zipper of her slacks.

The second Anna learned from the first and claimed to love sunshine and detest lies. It sounded like a translation of one of those Playmate of the Month data sheets, the answers always written in the same loopy handwriting: "Turn-ons: Mom's famous five-alarm chili! Turnoffs: insecurity and guys who come on too strong!!!!"

The two Polish Annas surely had clear notions of what they loved and hated, but like the rest of us, they were limited in terms of vocabulary, and this made them appear less than sophisticated. The teacher forged on, and we learned that Carlos, the Argentine bandonion player, loved wine, music, and, in his words, "making sex with the womens of the world." Next came a beautiful young Yugoslav who identified herself as an optimist, saying that she loved everything that life had to offer.

The teacher licked her lips, revealing a hint of the saucebox we would later come to know. She crouched low for her attack, placed her hands on the young woman's desk, and leaned close, saying, "Oh yeah? And do you love your little war?"

While the optimist struggled to defend herself, I scrambled to think of an answer to what had obviously become a trick question. How often is one asked what he loves in this world? More to the point, how often is one asked and then publicly ridiculed for his answer? I recalled my mother, flushed with wine, pounding the tabletop late one night, saying, "Love? I love a good steak cooked rare. I love my cat, and I love . . ." My sisters and I leaned forward, waiting to hear our names. "Tums," our mother said. "I love Tums."

The teacher killed some time accusing the Yugoslavian girl of masterminding a program of genocide, and I jotted frantic notes in the margins of my pad. While I can honestly say that I love leafing through medical textbooks devoted to severe dermatological conditions, the hobby is beyond the reach of my French vocabulary, and acting it out would only have invited controversy.

When called upon, I delivered an effortless list of things that I detest: blood sausage, intestinal pâtés, brain pudding. I'd learned these words the hard way. Having given it some thought, I then declared my love for IBM typewriters, the French word for *bruise*, and my electric floor waxer. It was a short list, but still I managed to mispronounce *IBM* and assign the wrong gender to both the floor waxer and the typewriter. The teacher's reaction led me to believe that these mistakes were capital crimes in the country of France.

"Were you always this *palicmkrexis*?" she asked. "Even a *fiuscrzsa ticiwelmun* knows that a typewriter is feminine."

I absorbed as much of her abuse as I could understand, thinking—but not saying—that I find it ridiculous to assign a gender to an inanimate object incapable of disrobing and making an occasional fool of itself. Why refer to Lady Crack Pipe or Good Sir Dishrag when these things could never live up to all that their sex implied?

The teacher proceeded to belittle everyone from German Eva, who hated laziness, to Japanese Yukari, who loved paintbrushes and soap. Italian, Thai, Dutch, Korean, and Chinese—we all left class foolishly believing that the worst was over. She'd shaken us up a little, but surely that was just an act designed to weed out the deadweight. We didn't know it then, but the coming months would teach us what it was like to spend time in the presence of a wild animal, something completely unpredictable. Her temperament was not based on a series of good and bad days but, rather, good and bad moments. We soon learned to dodge chalk and protect our heads and

EVEN A "FIUSCRZSA TICIWELMUN" KNOWS THAT A TYPEWRITER IS FEMININE.

stomachs whenever she approached us with a question. She hadn't yet punched anyone, but it seemed wise to protect ourselves against the inevitable.

Though we were forbidden to speak anything but French, the teacher would occasionally use us to practice any of her five fluent languages.

"I hate you," she said to me one afternoon. Her English was flawless. "I really, really hate you." Call me sensitive, but I couldn't help but take it personally.

After being singled out as a lazy *kfdtinvfm*, I took to spending four hours a night on my homework, putting in even more time whenever we were assigned an essay. I suppose I could have gotten by with less, but I was determined to create some sort of identity for myself: David the hard worker, David the cut-up. We'd have one of those "complete this sentence" exercises, and I'd fool with the thing for hours, invariably settling on something like "A quick run around the lake? I'd love to! Just give me a moment while I strap on my wooden leg." The teacher, through word and action, conveyed the message that if this was my idea of an identity, she wanted nothing to do with it.

My fear and discomfort crept beyond the borders of the classroom and accompanied me out onto the wide boulevards. Stopping for a coffee, asking directions, depositing money in my bank account: these things were out of the question, as they involved having to speak. Before beginning school, there'd been no shutting me up, but now I was convinced that everything I said was wrong. When the phone rang, I ignored it. If someone asked me a question, I pretended to be deaf. I knew my fear was getting the best of me when I started wondering why they don't sell cuts of meat in vending machines.

My only comfort was the knowledge that I was not alone. Huddled in the hallways and making the most of our pathetic French, my fellow students and I engaged in the sort of conversation commonly overheard in refugee camps.

"Sometime me cry alone at night."

"That be common for I, also, but be more strong, you. Much work and someday you talk pretty. People start love you soon. Maybe tomorrow, okay."

Unlike the French class I had taken in New York, here there was no sense of competition. When the teacher poked a shy Korean in the eyelid with a freshly sharpened pencil, we took no comfort in the fact that, unlike Hyeyoon Cho, we all knew the irregular past tense of the verb *to defeat*. In all fairness, the teacher hadn't meant to stab the girl, but neither did she spend much time apologizing, saying only, "Well, you should have been *vkkdyo* more *kdeynfulh*."

Over time it became impossible to believe that any of us would ever improve. Fall arrived and it rained every day, meaning we would now be scolded for the water dripping from our coats and umbrellas. It was mid-October when the teacher singled me out, saying, "Every day spent with you is like having a cesarean section." And it struck me that, for the first time since arriving in France, I could understand every word that someone was saying.

Understanding doesn't mean that you can suddenly speak the language. Far from it. It's a small step, nothing more, yet its rewards are intoxicating and deceptive. The teacher continued her diatribe and I settled back, bathing in the subtle beauty of each new curse and insult.

"You exhaust me with your foolishness and reward my efforts with nothing but pain, do you understand me?"

The world opened up, and it was with great joy that I responded, "I know the thing that you speak exact now. Talk me more, you, plus, please, plus."

Chocolat

Once I went to the Chocolate Show in Paris, which was held in a convention center beneath the Louvre. I like chocolate more than most, I guess (seeing as I was under the Louvre at the Chocolate Show instead of looking at the *Mona Lisa* upstairs), but I was shocked, then delighted, to see the Parisians tasting—then madly discussing—each morsel of cocoa they tried. I never thought of actually discussing chocolate before. They are passionate about food in general, but there seems to be a special place in their hearts for chocolate. Here are some mouthwatering bonbon shops.

LA CHARLOTTE DE L'ISLE (4è; Métro: Pont Marie or Cité; 24 rue Saint Louis en l'Île). Beyond the clever chocolates shaped as birds and bunnies found in this cluttered, homey shop, there is the heavenly hot chocolate.

JEAN-PAUL HÉVIN (1er; Métro: Concorde or Opéra; 231 rue Saint Honoré). Master pastry maker Jean-Paul Hévin was awarded Meilleur Ouvrier de France (best craftsman in France) in 1986—and his chocolates show it.

LA MAISON DU CHOCOLAT (9è; Métro: Madeleine; 8 blvd de la Madeleine). Chocolatier Robert Linxe strives for "chocolate without bitterness" by choosing the right cocoa bean; philosopher Jean-Paul Aron calls him "the wizard of ganache."

MICHEL CHAUDUN (7è; Métro: La Tour Maubourg or Invalides; 149 rue de l'Université). Less polished, more homemade looking, nine different sources of chocolate are blended to form the base of all Chaudun's chocolates; don't leave without trying the pavés and mini ganaches.

PIERRE HERMÉ (6è; Métro: Saint Sulpice; 72 rue Bonaparte). This is mostly a pastry shop—and they're really tempting too—but the chocolates are outstanding.

Cuckoo For Cocoa

The exclusive 150-member cocoa-savvy organization, Le Club des Croqueurs de Chocolat—who meet often at their headquarters in Paris to discuss all things chocolate—offer these guidelines:

Dark chocolate (without milk), our preferred choice, must have: A lustrous surface; a warm and velvety tint; a clean break; a deep and frank parfum of cacao; between 60% and 75% cacao; a long-lasting flavor on the tongue; a palatable bitter note with a touch of acidity.

ARRONDISSEMENT 14ÈME

Practically any artist you can name from the early 20th century lived, worked, and drank in Montparnasse, nicknamed for Mont Parnassus, home of Apollo, the god of poetry, music, and beauty. The 14th was bohemian central then, and this neighborhood is all about those artists (Hemingway, Picasso, Chagall, Léger), their gathering places, and even their graves. Because the living conditions were woeful at best, cafés were both the offices and meeting places of the talent. Le Dôme, La Closerie des Lilas, and La Coupole were three of the most popular (the owners would occasionally take drawings or paintings to cover the tab), and they are still in business today. Americans came in droves during the *années folles* (the crazy years), taking advantage of the weak franc and raising the expat population from 6,000 in 1921 to 30,000 in 1924.

All that came to a screeching halt during World War II, and never recovered. Still, spotting names in the Montparnasse cemetery such as Frédéric Bartholdi (creator of the Statue of Liberty), Simone de Beauvoir, Jean-Paul Sartre, Brassaï, Samuel Beckett, and Man Ray will remind you of what once was.

More—if less famous—dead can be viewed by climbing down into the nearby catacombs. When the old cemetery from les Halles was closed in 1786, the remains were put (in very orderly stacks) here. The entrance is across from the Denfert-Rochereau Métro station.

Today the Tour Montparnasse (a 56-story blah office tower) is the neighborhood's most outstanding landmark.

April in Paris

BY E. Y. HARBURG

April's in the air,
But here in Paris
April wears a different gown.
You can see her waltzing down the street.
The tang of wine is in the air,
I'm drunk with all the happiness that spring can give,
Never dreamed it could be so exciting to live.

April in Paris,
Chestnuts in blossom,
Holiday tables under the trees.
April in Paris
This is a feeling
No one can ever reprise.

I never knew the charm of spring,
Never met it face to face.
I never knew my heart could sing,
Never missed a warm embrace, till
April in Paris,

Je Suis Américaine . . .

Sculptor Frédéric-Auguste Bartholdi was at a small dinner party in 1865 when a political discussion broke out about the repressive regime of Napoleon III. The talk soon turned to America, which had just emerged—whole and slave-free—from a bloody Civil War. The small group admired America's love of liberty and constitutional government and, with the upcoming American centennial in mind, proposed that a gift be sent. Twenty-one years later, on a rainy October day, the Statue of Liberty—perhaps the most conspicuous Franco-American ever—was unveiled in New York Harbor.

Jessica Alba 🪦 Patricia Arquette ⚜ Rene Auberjonois 🪦 Kevyn Aucoin

John James Audubon 🪦 Lucille Ball 🪦 Adrienne Barbeau ⚜ Tom Bergeron

Kathleen Blanco ⚜ Anthony Bourdain 🪦 John Vernou Bouvier III

The Cadillac Family 🪦 Jim Carrey ⚜ James Carville 🪦 Lon Chaney

Robert Clary 🪦 Claudette Colbert 🪦 Stephen Colbert 🪦 Philippe Cousteau Jr.

Joan Crawford ⚜ Ann Danton-Liberator 🪦 Ellen DeGeneres ⚜ Tom DeLay

Johnny Depp ⚜ Wylie Dufresne 🪦 Leo Durocher 🪦 James Duval 🪦 Nanette Fabray

Brett Favre ⚜ Robert Goulet 🪦 Ron Guidry ⚜ Alexander Hamilton ⚜ Anne Hathaway

Dan Ingram 🪦 Angelina Jolie ⚜ Caroline Kennedy 🪦 John F. Kennedy

John F. Kennedy Jr. 🪦 Jack Kerouac 🪦 Beyoncé Knowles ⚜ Nick Lachey

Jean Lafitte ⚜ Emeril Lagasse 🪦 Jack LaLanne 🪦 Dorothy Lamour ⚜ Tom Landry

Lyndon LaRouche 🪦 Matt LeBlanc 🪦 Julia Louis-Dreyfus 🪦 Yo-Yo Ma 🪦 Madonna

Tammy Faye Messner 🪦 Grace Metalious 🪦 Liza Minnelli ⚜ Anaïs Nin

Bill Nye 🪦 Jacqueline Kennedy Onassis ⚜ Andy Pettitte 🪦 Lily Pons 🪦 Annie Proulx

Paul Prudhomme 🪦 Paul Revere 🪦 The Rockefeller Family (originally Roquefeuille)

Felix Rohatyn 🪦 Pierre Salinger ⚜ Oliver Stone ⚜ Charlize Theron 🪦 Paul Theroux

Henry David Thoreau 🪦 Garry Trudeau 🪦 Paul Tulane ⚜ Robin Williams

ARRONDISSEMENT 15ÈME

Excluding the Bois de Boulogne and the Bois de Vincennes (the wooded areas that abut the 16th and 12th arrondissements), the 15th is the largest and most populated of the 20 arrondissements. Although this neighborhood is mostly residential today, it has a very industrial past. Quarries (around Vaugirard), chemical manufacturers (bleach or *eau de Javel* was invented here), and Citroën (the car company) had factories here until the 1970s. They have since been replaced by TV studios, including the multinational producer Canal+.

Part of Montparnasse also spills into the 15th, and that area was home to many artists in the early 20th century. La Ruche, a legendary warren of ateliers and living spaces for painters, writers, and sculptors, was home to Marc Chagall, Léger, Max Jacob, Modigliani, Brancusi, and Diego Rivera, among others. Created out of the scraps left over from the 1900 World Exposition (like the Indian and Bordeaux wine pavilions designed by Gustav Eiffel), the round building was divided like "an evil brie cheese," according to French/Russian painter-sculptor Ossip Zadkine.

The French chemist Louis Pasteur, who is best known for inventing the process that keeps milk from going bad, lived and worked here in the 19th century, and his apartment/atelier has been made into a museum housing a collection of scientific souvenirs along with his crypt.

The architectural oddity of the neighborhood (considering the uniformity of Paris) is the Front de Seine, a district of mixed residential-commercial high-rise (12–32 stories) buildings.

Bourgeois dogs in the neighborhood love the freshly baked "gourmet" dog biscuits at Mon Bon Chien (12 rue Mademoiselle). Try the foie gras or boeuf barbecue!

TO MISS LUCY CRANCH

Auteuil, 5 September, 1784

from Abigail Adams

My Dear Lucy,

. . . You inquire of me how I like Paris. Why, they tell me I
am no judge, for that I have not seen it yet. One thing, I
know, and that is that I have smelt it. If I was agreeably disappointed in London, I am as much disappointed in Paris.
It is the very dirtiest place I ever saw. There are some buildings and some squares, which are tolerable; but in general
the streets are narrow, the shops, the houses, inelegant and
dirty, the streets full of lumber and stone, with which they
build. Boston cannot boast so elegant public buildings;
but, in every other respect, it is as much superior in my
eyes to Paris, as London is to Boston. To have had Paris
tolerable to me, I should not have gone to London. As to
the people here, they are more given to hospitality than in
England it is said. I have been in company with but one
French lady since I arrived; for strangers here make the
first visit, and nobody will know you until you have waited upon them in form.

This lady I dined with at Dr. Franklin's. She entered

the room with a careless, jaunty air; upon seeing ladies who were strangers to her, she bawled out, "Ah! mon Dieu, where is Franklin? Why did you not tell me there were ladies here?" You must suppose her speaking all this in French. "How I look!" said she, taking hold of a chemise made of tiffany, which she had on over a blue lute-string, and which looked as much upon the decay as her beauty, for she was once a handsome women; her hair was frizzled; over it she had a small straw hat, with a dirty gauze half-handkerchief round it, and a bit of dirtier gauze, than ever my maids wore, was bowed on behind. She had a black gauze scarf thrown over her shoulders. She ran out of the room; when she returned, the Doctor entered at one door, she at the other; upon which she ran forward to him, caught him by the hand, "Helas! Franklin;" then gave him a double kiss, one upon each cheek, and another upon his forehead. When we went into the room to dine, she was placed between the Doctor and Mr. Adams. She carried on the chief of the conversation at dinner, frequently locking her hand into the Doctor's, and sometimes spreading her arms upon the backs of both the gentlemen's chairs, then throwing her arm carelessly upon the Doctor's neck.

I should have been greatly astonished at this conduct, if the good Doctor had not told me that in this lady I should see a genuine Frenchwoman, wholly free from affectation or stiffness of behaviour, and one of the best women in the world. For this I must take the Doctor's word; but I should have set her down for a very bad one, although sixty years of age, and a widow. I own I was highly disgusted, and never wish for an acquaintance with any ladies of this cast. After dinner she threw herself upon a settee, where she showed more than her feet. She had a little lap-dog, who was, next to the Doctor, her favorite. This she kissed, and when he wet the floor, she wiped it up with her chemise. This is one of the Doctor's most intimate friends, with whom he dines once every week, and she with him. She is rich, and is my near neighbour; but I have not yet visited her. Thus you see, my dear, that manners differ exceedingly in different countries. I hope, however, to find amongst the French ladies manners more consistent with my ideas of decency, or I shall be a mere recluse.

You must write to me, and let me know all about you; marriages, births, and preferments; every thing you can think of. Give my respects to the Germantown family. I shall begin to get letters from them by the nest vessel.

Good night. Believe me

Your most affectionate aunt, A. A.

ARRONDISSEMENT 16ÈME

Ben Franklin lived in this wealthy and conservative neighborhood—then part of the village of Passy, conveniently located between Paris and Versailles—for nearly 10 years as America's first diplomat. Occasionally he would cross the river to help send up experimental balloons from the Champs de Mars (where the Eiffel Tower now stands). This upscale neighborhood is still home to many international embassies.

Of course, the most famous site in the 16th is the Arc de Triomphe. But you can also find a replica of the flame of the Statue of Liberty, the Palais de Tokyo museum, and an amazing art nouveau enclave here— architectural diamonds among the glittering neighborhood including Guimard's masterpiece Castel Béranger (14 rue la Fontaine). There is an exceptional view of both the Arc de Triomphe and the Eiffel Tower from the terrace of the restaurant Les Jardins Plein Ciel (17 ave Kléber), which is on the seventh floor of the Hôtel Raphaël.

This, the westernmost arrondissement, is also where tennis stars battle it out on the clay courts of Roland Garros Stadium, home to the French Open.

Befitting the neighborhood, the Musée Baccarat, designed by Philippe Starck in a sumptuous mansion that once belonged to the Viscountess Marie Laure de Noailles, pays homage to the famous leaded-glass maker. Glittery jewelry, lighting, and glassware are on display, while the Baccarat Cristal Room, a really expensive restaurant, provides refreshment. There is a gift shop.

Arc de Triomphe

Right in the middle of a fascinating yet maddening confluence of 12 major avenues—and the *grand-mère* of all roundabouts—stands one of the most impressive triumphal arches in the world. This monument in celebration of war—with a nod to peace—was designed to mark Napoleon's great victory at Austerlitz in 1805. Unfortunately Napoleon met up with Wellington at Waterloo in 1815 and was finished long before the arch was. Though Napoleon's army never passed by in celebration, several others have over the years: Germans (1871), French (1918), Germans again (1940), Free French forces, and the Allies (1944).

One of the most important gatherings in recent times was in celebration of France's victory over Brazil to win 1998's World Cup. Over a million fans turned out and danced until dawn on the Champs-Élysées with the arch as backdrop.

A 1758 cross section of L'Éléphant Triomphal, engineer Charles Ribart's fountain/ballroom monument that was designed to stand in the park where the Arc de Triomphe is now.

Benjamin Franklin
(1706–1790)

When Benjamin Franklin first set foot in Paris, on a visit in 1767, his reputation as an electrician—which meant scientist in those days rather than technician—preceded him, and helped open the door to meeting many influential Parisians, including King Louis XV.

The connections he made then came in handy when he was sent back to France nine years later as ambassador from the brand-new United States. His assignment then—during the American Revolution—was to procure supplies (guns, uniforms, shoes) for the war along with the money to buy them.

Lucky for America he took Paris by storm as a kind of countrified royalty from the New World. In the fine-lace-and-embroidery court of Louis XVI (and Marie Antoinette), he showed up in his cloddish (but charming) fur hat and spectacles. The public was enamored; soon ladies were wearing their hair styled to imitate his fur hat and carrying around his portrait on snuffboxes.

His powers of persuasion eventually won French support (they sent guns, cannons, and cash), and France became the first country to formally recognize the existence of the United States.

Franklin lived in what was then the suburb Passy (in the 16th arrondissement) where, in his spare time, he learned French, flirted with many Parisiennes, and watched (with great fascination) the Montgolfier brothers launch their new technology, the hot-air balloon.

Other patriots in Paris: John Adams, Thomas Jefferson, Thomas Paine.

TO MARY STEVENSON

Paris, September 14, 1767

from Benjamin Franklin

Dear Polly

I am always pleas'd with a Letter from you, and I flatter myself you may be sometimes pleas'd in receiving one from me, tho' it should be of little Importance, such as this, which is to consist of a few occasional Remarks made here and in my Journey hither.

Various Impositions we suffer'd from Boat-men, Porters, &c. on both Sides the Water. I know not which are most rapacious, the English or French; but the latter have, with their Knavery the most Politeness.

The Roads we found equally good with ours in England, in some Places pave'd with smooth Stone like our new Streets for many Miles together, and Rows of Trees on each Side and yet there are no Turnpikes. But then the poor Peasants complain'd to us grievously, that they were oblig'd to work upon the Roads full two Months in the Year without being paid for their Labour: Whether this is Truth, or whether, like Englishmen, they grumble Cause or no Cause, I have not yet been able fully to inform myself.

. . . The Civilities we every where receive give us the strongest Impressions of the French Politeness. It seems to be a

TO MARY STEVENSON

Point settled here universally that Strangers are to be treated with Respect, and one has just the same Deference shewn one here by being a Stranger as in England by being a Lady. The Custom House Officers at Port St. Denis, as we enter'd Paris, were about to seize 2 Doz. of excellent Bourdeaux Wine given us at Boulogne, and which we brought with us; but as soon as they found we were Strangers, it was immediately remitted on that Account. At the Church of Notre Dame, when we went to see a magnificent Illumination with Figures &c. for the deceas'd Dauphiness, we found an immense Croud who were kept out by Guards; but the Officer being told that we were Strangers from England, he immediately admitted us, accompanied and show'd us every thing. Why don't we practise this Urbanity to Frenchmen? Why should they be allow'd to out-do us in any thing?

Here is an Exhibition of Paintings, &c. like ours in London, to which Multitudes flock daily. I am not Connoisseur enough to judge which has most Merit. Every Night, Sundays not excepted here are Plays or Operas; and tho' the Weather has been hot, and the Houses full, one is not incommoded by the Heat so much as with us in Winter. They must have some Way of changing the Air that we are not acquainted with. I shall enquire into it.

Travelling is one Way of lengthening Life, at least in

TO MARY STEVENSON

Appearance. It is but a Fortnight since we left London; but the Variety of Scenes we have gone through makes it seem equal to Six Months living in one Place. Perhaps I have suffered a greater Change too in my own Person than I could have done in Six Years at home. I had not been here Six Days before my Taylor and Peruquier had transform'd me into a Frenchman. Only think what a Figure I make in a little Bag Wig and naked Ears! They told me I was become 20 Years younger, and look'd very galante; so being in Paris where the Mode is to be sacredly follow'd, I was once very near making Love to my Friend's Wife.

This Letter shall cost you a Shilling, and you may think it cheap when you consider that it has cost me at least 50 Guineas to get into the Situation that enables me to write it. Besides, I might, if I had staid at home, heave won perhaps two shillings of you at Cribbidge. By the Way, now I mention Cards, let me tell you that Quadrille is quite out of Fashion here, and English Whisk all the Mode, at Paris and the Court.

And pray look upon it as no small Matter, that surrounded as I am by the Glories of this World and Amusements of all Sorts, I remember you and Dolly and all the dear good Folks at Bromley. 'Tis true I can't help it, but must and ever shall remember you all with Pleasure. Need I add that I am particularly, my dear good Friend Yours most affectionately.

ARRONDISSEMENT 17ÈME

This is the neighborhood that first saw the Statue of Liberty. From 1882 through 1884 the Atelier Monduit et Béchet—the foundry on rue Chazelles—cast the statue's copper sections. During construction, a walk past the atelier became a favorite promenade for Parisians.

Baron Haussmann, who saw the area as the perfect place to build for the up-and-coming middle class, replaced the cornfields and hunting grounds with inexpensive housing that lured the impressionists, who flocked here at the end of the 19th century for the cheap rents and abundant sunlight (it was they who eschewed the tradition of painting indoors). Typically Edouard Manet would hold court every Thursday with Zola, Degas, Monet, and Renoir at the Café Guerbois. Today the neighborhood remains primarily working class.

Some great chocolate can be drunk (cocktails), eaten (mousse), and most deliciously inhaled at Puerto Cacao (53 rue de Tocqueville), an ethical (organic, socially responsible) chocolatier in the neighborhood. Happy hour is between 2 and 5 PM.

THE BIG SEA

by Langston Hughes

MONTMARTRE

My ticket and the French visa had taken nearly all my money. I got to the Gare du Nord in Paris early one February morning with only seven dollars in my pockets. I didn't know anybody in the whole of Europe, except the old Dutch watchman's family in Rotterdam. But I had made up my mind to pass the rest of the winter in Paris.

I checked my bags at the parcel stand, and had some coffee and rolls in the station. I found that my high school French didn't work very well, and that I understood nothing anyone said to me. They talked too fast. But I could read French.

I went outside the station and saw a bus marked *Opéra*. I knew the opera was at the center of Paris, so I got in the bus and rode down there, determined to do a little sight-seeing before I looked for work, or maybe starved to death. When I got to the Opéra, a fine wet snow was falling. People were pouring out of the Métro on their way to work. To the right and left of me stretched the Grands Boulevards. I looked across the street and saw the Café de la Paix. Ahead the Vendôme. I walked down the rue de la Paix, turned, and on until I came out at the Concorde. I recognized the Champs Elysées, and the great Arc de Triomphe in the distance through the snow.

Boy, was I thrilled! I was torn between walking up the Champs Elysées or down along the Seine, past the Tuileries. Finally, I took the river, hoping to see the bookstalls and Notre Dame. But I ended up in the Louvre instead, looking at Venus.

It was warmer in the Louvre than in the street, and the Greek statues were calm and friendly. I said to the statues: "If you can stay in Paris as long as you've been here and still look O.K., I guess I can stay a while with seven dollars and make a go of it." But when I came out of the Louvre, I was tired and hungry. I had no idea where I would sleep that night, or where to go about finding a cheap hotel. So I began to look around for someone I could talk to. To tell the truth, I began to look for a colored person on the streets of Paris.

As luck would have it, I came across an American Negro in a doorman's uniform. He told me most of the American colored people he knew lived in Montmartre, and that they were musicians working in the theaters and night clubs. He directed me to Montmartre. I walked. I passed Notre Dame de Lorette, then on up the hill. I got to Montmartre about four o'clock. Many of the people there were just getting up and having their breakfast at that hour, since they worked all night. I don't think they were in a very good humor, because I went into a little café where I saw some colored musicians sitting, having their coffee. I spoke to them, and said: "I've just come to Paris, and I'm looking for a cheap place to stay and a job."

They scowled at me. Finally one of them said: "Well, what instrument do you play?"

They thought I was musical competition.

I said: "None. I'm just looking for an ordinary job."

Puzzled, another one asked: "Do you tap dance, or what?"

"No," I said, "I've just got off a ship and I want any kind of a job there is."

"You must be crazy, boy," one of the men said. "There ain't no 'any kind of job' here. There're plenty of French people for ordinary work. 'Less you can play jazz or tap dance, you'd just as well go back home."

"He's telling you right," the rest of the fellows at the table agreed, "there's no work here."

But one of them indicated a hotel. "Go over there across the street and see if you can't get a little room cheap."

I went. But it was high for me, almost a dollar a day in American money. However, I had to take the room for that night. Then I ate my first dinner in Paris—*bœuf au gros sel,* and a cream cheese with sugar. Even with the damp and the slush—for the snow had turned to a nasty rain—I began to like Paris a little, and to take it personally.

The next day I went everywhere where people spoke English, looking for a job—the American Library, the Embassy, the American Express, the newspaper offices. Nothing doing. Besides I would have to have a *carte d'identité.* But it would be better to go back home, I was advised, because there were plenty of people out of work in Paris.

"With five dollars, I can't go back home," I said.

People shrugged their shoulders and went on doing whatever they were doing. I tramped the streets. Late afternoon of the second day came. I went back to Montmartre, to that same little café in front of my hotel, where I had no room that night—unless I paid again. And if I did take the same room again, with supper, I'd have scarcely four dollars left!

My bags were still checked at the station, so I had no clean clothes to put on. It was drizzling rain, and I was cold and hungry. I had had only coffee and a roll all day. I felt bad.

I slumped down at a table in the

small café and ordered another *café crème* and a *croissant*—the second that day. I ate the croissant (a slender, curved French roll) and wondered what on earth I ought to do. I decided tomorrow to try the French for a job somewhere, maybe the Ritz or some other of the large hotels, or maybe where I had seen them building a big building on one of the boulevards. Perhaps they could use a hodcarrier.

The café had begun to be crowded, as the afternoon darkened into a damp and murky dusk. A tall, young colored fellow came in and sat down at the marble-topped table where I was. He ordered a *fine,* and asked me if I wanted to play dominoes.

I said no, I was looking for a cheap room.

He recommended his hotel, where he lived by the month, but when we figured it out, it was about the same as the place across the street, too high for me. I said I meant a *really* cheap room.

I said I didn't care about heat or hot water or carpets on the floor right now, just a place to sleep. He said he didn't know of any hotels like that, as cheap as I needed.

Just then a girl, with reddish-blond hair, sitting on a bench that ran along the wall, spoke up and said: "You say you look at one hotel?"

I said: "Yes."

She said: "I know one, not much dear."

"Where?" I asked her. "And how much?"

"Almost not nothing," she said, "not dear! No! I will show you. Come."

She put on her thin coat and got up. I followed her. She was a short girl, with a round, pale Slavic face and big dark eyes. She had a little rouge on her cheeks. She had on a wine-red hat with a rain-wilted feather. She was pretty, but her slippers were worn at the heels. We walked up the hill in silence, across the Place Blanche and up

What a winter that one of 1929 was! Paris in white velvet, all the windows like moonstones.

—Max Jacob

toward the rue Lepic. Finally I said to her, in French, that I had very little money and the room would have to be very cheap or I would have nothing left to eat on, because I had no *travaille*. No *travaille* and no prospects, and I was not a musician.

She answered that this was the cheapest hotel in Montmartre, where she was taking me. *"Pas de tout cher."* But, as she spoke, I could tell that her French was almost as bad as mine, so we switched back to English, which she spoke passably well.

She said she had not been in Paris long, that she had come from Constantinople with a ballet troupe, and that she was Russian. Beyond that, she volunteered no information. The drizzling February rain wet our faces, the water was soggy in my shoes, and the girl looked none too warm in her thin but rather chic coat. After several turns up and down a narrow, winding street, we came to the hotel, a tall,

neat-looking building, with a tiled entrance hall. From a tiny sitting room came a large French woman. And the girl spoke to her about the room, the very least dear, for *m'sieu*.

"Oui," said the woman, "a quite small room, by the week, fifty francs."

"I'll take it," I said, "and pay two weeks." I knew it would leave me almost nothing, but I would have a place to sleep.

I thanked the girl for bringing me to the hotel and I invited her to a cup of coffee with me next time we met at the café. We parted at the Place Blanche, and I went to the station to get my bags, now that I had some place to put them. After paying for the room and the storage of my bags, I had just about enough money left for coffee and rolls for a week—if I ate nothing *but* coffee and one roll a meal.

I was terribly hungry and it took me some time to get to the station by Métro. I got back to the hotel about nine that night, through a chilly drizzle. My key was not hanging on the hallboard, but the landlady pointed up, so I went up. It was a long climb with the bags, and I stopped on each landing to rest. I guess I was weak with hunger, having only eaten those two croissants all day. When I got to my room, I could see a light beneath the door, so I thought maybe I was confused about the number. I hesitated, then knocked. The door opened and there stood the Russian girl.

I said: "Hello!"

I didn't know what else to say.

She said: "I first return me," and smiled.

Her coat was hanging on a nail behind the door and a small bag sat beneath the window. She was barefooted, her wet shoes were beneath the heatless radiator, and her stockings drying on the foot of the bed.

I said: "Are you going to stay here, too?"

She said: "Of course! *Mais oui!* Why you think, I find one room?"

She had her hat off. Her red-blond hair was soft and wavy. She laughed and laughed. I laughed, too, since I didn't know what to say.

"I have no mon-nee nedder," she said.

We sat down on the bed. In broken English, she told me her story. Her name was Sonya. Her dancing troupe had gone to pieces in Nice. She had bought a ticket to Paris. And here we were—in a room that was all bed, just space barely to open the door, that was all, and a few nails in the barren wall, on which to hang clothes. No heat in the radiator. No table, no washstand, no chair, but a deep window seat that could serve as a chair and a place to put things on. It was cold, so cold you could see your breath. But the rent was cheap, so you couldn't ask for much.

We didn't ask for anything.

I put my suitcase under the bed.

Sonya hung her clothes on the nails. She said: "If you have some francs I go *chez l'épicerie* and get white cheese and one small bread and one small wine and we have supper. Eat right here. That way are less dear."

I gave her ten francs and she went out shopping for the supper. We spread the food on the bed. It tasted very good and cost little, cheese and crisp, fresh bread and a bottle of wine. But I could see my francs gone in a few days more. Then what would we do? But Sonya said she was looking for a job, and perhaps she would find one soon, then we both could eat.

Not being accustomed to the quick friendship of the dispossessed, I wondered if she meant it. Later, I knew she did. She found a job first. And we both ate.

WORK

Sonya found work as a danseuse at Zelli's famous night club in the rue Fontaine. Not as a dancer in the show, but as a dancer with patrons—a girl who sits at tables, dances with the guests and persuades them to order one more drink—and then another— usually champagne. She got no pay, but drew a commission on every bottle of champagne, beyond the first, she could persuade a guest to buy. Result, she drank a great many glasses of champagne every night, because the faster she could aid a bottle of champagne to disappear, the sooner a new one would appear, and like lightning, be opened by the attentive waiters, with an additional commission added in Sonya's column at the *caisse*.

. . .

And still there was no letter from my mother in McKeesport, much less a cable for twenty dollars. Finally, when a letter did arrive from home, it contained the longest list of calamities I have ever seen on one sheet of paper.

In the first place, my mother wrote, my step-father was seriously ill in the city hospital with pneumonia; she herself had no job and no money; my little brother had been expelled from school for fighting; and besides all that, the river was rising in McKeesport. The water was already knee-deep at the door, and if it got any higher she would have to get a rowboat and move out of the house. The Jewish people downstairs had fled to stay with relatives. But my mother had no place to go, and she couldn't even send me a two-cent stamp, much less twenty dollars. Besides, what was I doing way over there in France? Why didn't I stay home like decent folks, get a job, and go to work and help her—instead of galavanting all over the world as a sailor, and writing from Paris for money?

Well, I felt bad. I wondered how I would ever get back home, and how my mother would get along with so much trouble on her hands.

Fortunately, a few days after that letter came, I got a job myself. I had tried all the big night clubs in Montmartre, now I decided to try the little ones; so I started out early one evening. I noticed a little club in the rue Fontaine that had no doorman. I went in and asked for the owner. The owner turned out to be a colored woman, a *Martiniquaise*. I addressed her politely in my best French and asked if she needed a *chausseur*. She looked at me a moment, and finally said: *"Oui! Cinq francs et le dîner."* Naturally, I accepted.

Then and there, she showed me

the way to the kitchen, where the cook fed me. And at ten o'clock that night, I took up my post outside the door on the rue Fontaine. The heavy dinner the cook gave me and the big bottle of wine that went with it made me so sleepy that I went to sleep standing up in the street outside the door. I couldn't help it. I slept almost all night.

I had no uniform, but the next day, at the Flea Market, I bought a blue cap with gold braid on it, which gave me an air of authority. My salary, five francs a night, was less than a quarter in American money, but it was a great help in Paris until I could do better.

Shortly after I began working for the Martinique lady, Sonya secured a contract to dance at Le Havre, so one rainy March afternoon I went to the Gare St. Lazare with her to say good-bye. She cried and I felt bad seeing her cry. She had been a swell friend and I liked her. She waved at me through the window as the long train pulled out. I

waved back. And I never saw her any more.

That night I felt lonesome and sad standing outside the door of the little *boîte* in the cold, damp, winter night, my collar turned up and my cap with the gold braid pulled down as far over my ears as it would come. Every so often, I would step inside the door to get warm. Business was dull.

It was a very small night club of not more than ten tables and a tiny bar. There was a little Tzigane orchestra, and one entertainer. And a great many fights in the place.

Since they sold no cigarettes, the way I made my tips was largely by going to the corner to the *tabac* for packages of smokes for the guests. But whenever a fight would break out, I made an especial point of heading for the tabac so that I would not be called upon to stop it. I didn't know when I took the job that I was expected to be a bouncer as well as a doorman, and I didn't like the task of fight-stopping, because the first fight I saw there was between ladies, who shattered champagne glasses on the edge of the table, then slashed at each other with the jagged stems.

Madame's friend was a tall Roumanian girl, with large green circles painted on her eyes, who often came to the club in a white riding habit, white boots and hat, carrying a black whip. And madame herself would fight if the girl were insulted by any of the guests. For such a job, five francs was not enough, and the fights were too much, so I was glad when I found other work. Rayford Logan told me about an opening at a popular club on the rue Pigalle.

Rayford Logan is now a professor of history at Howard University in Washington. Then, he had been in France since the war, one of the Negro officers who stayed over there instead of coming home. That winter he was around Montmartre on crutches, having broken his leg in a bus accident. He received the *Crisis* all the time in Paris, and had read my poems, so when he knew I was a poet, he tried to help me find a job. One day he sent for me to tell me they needed a second cook at the Grand Duc, a well-known night club.

I couldn't cook, but I decided to say I could. Fortunately the title, second cook, really meant dishwasher, so I got the job. They fired another boy to give it to me. Strangely enough, the other boy happened to be from Cleveland, too, a tall brownskin fellow named Bob. He was discharged, the bosses said, because he came late to work, was unreliable, broke too many dishes, and cussed out the proprietors.

Gene Bullard, the colored manager, told me to be at work at eleven o'clock. Salary, fifteen francs a night and breakfast.

I was coming up in the world.

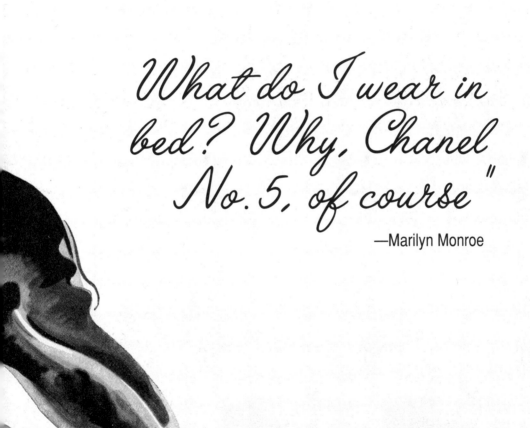

What do I wear in bed? Why, Chanel No. 5, of course "

—Marilyn Monroe

La Mode

New York, London, Milan . . . yes, high fashion bounces among these world capitals, but, thanks in part to the whims of Louis XIV and his style-conscious court who seemed to have started the trend, and Rose Bertin, Marie Antoinette's favored dressmaker (dubbed "Minister of Fashion") who continued pushing the envelope, Paris is fashion's hometown.

COCO CHANEL (1893–1971). Gabrielle Bonheur Chanel was taught to sew by nuns at the orphanage and picked up her nickname Coco while performing as a cabaret singer in 1905. She opened her first shop—making hats for famous actresses—in 1910 and went on to build a fashion empire. The Chanel signature style came about when she replaced the stiff and uncomfortable corset with simple, wearable (and *très chic*) clothes. She invented the little black dress, Chanel No. 5 perfume, and the quilted bag with shoulder strap.

CHRISTIAN DIOR (1905–1957). Dior opened an art gallery then sold fashion sketches to *Le Figaro*. He later worked as head designer at Robert Piguet and Lucien Lelong before opening his haute couture house in 1946 at 30 Avenue Montaigne. He invented the New Look, which was responsible for reigniting Paris's haute couture industry after World War II.

YVES SAINT LAURENT (b. 1936). Born in Algeria, Saint Laurent began working for Dior at 17 and was put in charge—to great success—upon Dior's death only four years later. He left Dior to start his own house with financier Pierre Bergé in 1962 and became known for mixing haute couture with a street-wise sense. He invented the androgynous-looking "le smoking" women's tuxedo, the sheer blouse, the jumpsuit, and designer ready-to-wear.

JEAN-PAUL GAULTIER (b. 1952). Gaultier had no formal design training but was hired by Pierre Cardin in 1970 after showing his sketches to Cardin. Six years later he presented his first collection. His style is one with a focus on pop culture. Even his haute couture line has a fun and playful side. He invented Madonna's look for the Blond Ambition tour in 1990 (yes, that look—with the huge cone bra).

EDITION SPÉCIALE COLLECTIONS 150 MODÈLES

LE TRIOMPHE CARDIN

LA
MODE
GAGNE

D'UNE

NGUEUR

NSIEUR J.M
SE LANCE
A HAUTE COUTURE

LE STYLE
J.M

MARQUE DES POINTS

(DE MODE)

L'ÉTERNEL CHANEL

LE CAS DIOR

Fashion passes;
style remains.

—Coco Chanel

Restez un Peu

The good news is that there are more than 150,000 rooms to choose from in the French capital. The bad news is, that's a lot of rooms. And some of them, like the Belle Étoile suite at Le Meurice—which I'm sure is very nice—can go for over $16,000 . . . per night! That works out great if you just won the lottery, but until then, here are some options that, while not deluxe, are still delovely.

Bon Marché (bargains)

CARON DE BEAUMARCHAIS (4è; Métro: Hôtel de Ville; 12 rue Vielle du Temple; +33 (0)1 42 72 34 12; carondebeaumarchais.com; 125–162€). The top-floor room in this hotel, located in the center of the Marais, with its ancient beams and balcony facing the street, may be small, but it is ever-so-romantic.

HÔTEL DES GRANDES ECOLES (5è; Métro: Cardinal Lemoine, place Monge or Jussieu; 75 rue Cardinal Lemoine; +33 (0)1 43 26 79 23; hotel-grandes-ecoles.com; 110–135€). This very wall-papery hotel is located just behind the Panthéon in the heart of the Latin Quarter where "each paving store is charged with history." Book early since the 51 rooms are constantly in demand.

HÔTEL MUGUET (7è; Métro: Ecole Militaire; 11 rue Chevert; +33 (0)1 47 05 05 93; paris-hotel-muguet.com; 100–180€). Named for the flower lily-of-the-valley, a traditional French good-luck charm and symbol of happiness, this simple, comfortable hotel is within walking distance of the Eiffel Tower.

NEW ORIENT HOTEL (8è; Métro: Europe, Rome, or Saint Lazare; 16 rue de Constantinople; +33 (0)1 45 22 21 64; hotel-paris-orient.com; 85–135€). A cozy room, steps from the Parc Monceau in a residential neighborhood, free Wi-Fi (pronounced "wee-fee")—*c'est super*.

À Louer (rentals)

RENTING an apartment is a good idea if you want to live like a local, are staying a long time, or are traveling with kids and you don't need the service a hotel offers. Pad à Terre (+33 (0)1 42 77 92 10; pad-a-terre.com) or Paris Attitude (+33 (0)1 42 96 31 46; parisattitude.com) are two great places to start your search.

ARRONDISSEMENT 18ÈME

The 18th arrondissement is one of both sinners and saints.

As with many of the arrondissements on the outskirts of the city, innkeepers and taverns set up shop just outside city gates to avoid taxes, and Parisians would partake of drink and entertainment at a discount. The tradition of both partying and praying on Montmartre goes back at least to the Romans, who built a temple to Bacchus (the god of wine) on the hill. And in the 12th century a Benedictine abbey was founded (thus the Métro station Abbesses), and the nuns, who had a wine press, went into business—a very lucrative one. All that ended badly, however, when the frail, blind, and deaf mother superior was sent to the guillotine during the revolution. A sad but fitting story from the "mount of martyrs."

Somehow, though, the two traditions continue. The Moulin Rouge, the tawdry Pigalle, the Erotic Museum are all here, but so is Sacré-Coeur, the 19th-century meringue confection overlooking Paris. Today the basilica is surrounded by artists chasing tourists and turning out goofy charcoal sketches, and while wine is still made on Montmartre, it has an abominable reputation. As for entertainment, at the corner of rue Saint Vincent and rue des Saules is a small, dilapidated, century-and-a-half-old cabaret called the Lapin Agile where you can drink the traditional cherries in brandy and sing all the old chansons like Picasso and Toulouse-Lautrec did in days gone by.

On October 1872 the archbishop of Paris was said to have had a vision while climbing the stairs of Montmartre and decided that there, "where the martyrs are," is where the Sacred Heart Basilica should be built. But Sacré-Coeur was not the first sanctuary on this hill overlooking Paris. The Druids prayed there, the Romans built a temple to Bacchus there, and Montmartre (literally martyr mountain) was named for Saint Denis (the patron saint of Paris), who was beheaded there while trying to convert the Gauls. But—martyr that he was—the loss of his head didn't stop him. He simply picked it up and walked out of town, delivering a sermon along the way.

312 PARIS — La Basilique du Sacré-Cœur et le Funiculaire — A. P. "Sacré-Cœur" basilic and funicular

Clad in travertine, a self-bleaching stone, this Romanesque-Byzantine bonbon contains one of Europe's largest mosaics, has the world's heaviest bell, and, from the dome, provides one of the greatest views of Paris.

The Basilica of the ridiculous.
—Emile Zola

While not really a monument, the name (meaning red windmill) and exterior of this—perhaps the world's best-known nightclub—have certainly become an established site in Paris. Opened in October 1889, the cabaret makes distinct references to the neighborhood's traditions both as an entertainment venue and as a windmill. The windmill atop the building is a kitsch nod to the rural origins of the neighborhood (where windmills spun until 1878), and the nightclub itself homage to the myriad entertainments found in Montmartre during the time it was located outside the walls of Paris (and thus immune to the city taxes on wine). In 1729, 134 out of 165 business in Montmartre were taverns or cabarets playing host to a motley crew of laborers, soldiers, and the occasional bandit.

By the time the Moulin Rouge opened, however, there was a more mixed clientele on the hill. Social mores began to relax after the Franco-Prussian War, and the bourgeois joined the riffraff on Montmartre looking for some naughty fun.

The Moulin Rouge's true heyday came at the turn of the 20th century. Mistinguette—known as Queen of the Music Hall—reigned, the cancan was having a revival, and scandal was à la mode.

Not much has changed in this burlesque palace since then—long legs still do very high kicks, breasts are bared, champagne flows, and lots of feathers fly nightly.

France is the thriftiest of all nations; to a Frenchman sex provides the most economical way to have fun. The French are a logical race. —Anita Loos

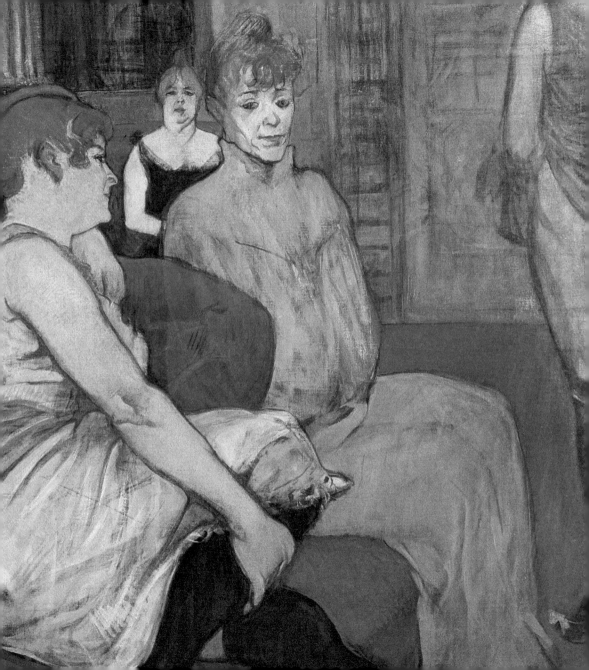

The Moulin Rouge
(Au Cinéma)

The Moulin Rouge has made an appearance in many films, or at least in the title of many. *Voilà une petite liste:*

QUEEN OF THE MOULIN ROUGE *(1922). Martha Mansfield and Joseph Striker star in this comedy involving a violin student, a dancer, and the French mob.*

LE FANTÔME DU MOULIN ROUGE *(1925). This French silent horrorish film finds Paris besieged by a ghost as the police try to track down the phantom's dead body.*

MOULIN ROUGE *(1928). This silent film from the UK concerns a mother–daughter–young lover triangle starring Olga Tschechowa (who was a "personal friend" of Adolf Hitler) as the singer-dancer mother, Eve Gray as the daughter, and Jean Bradin as the one in between, all with the Moulin Rouge as backdrop.*

MOULIN ROUGE *(1934). Constance Bennett plays twin French showgirls—one married to Franchot Tone's character, who does not want his wife in show business, and the other still dancing. They switch places in a plot that foreshadows an* I Love Lucy *episode . . . look for a young Lucille Ball in the chorus.*

MOULIN ROUGE *(1944)*. *A recut, reshot, and heavily censored American version of the 1935 French film* Princess Tam Tam *starring Josephine Baker. This version reduces Baker to a bit player and cuts out all interracial love scenes.*

DING-DONG: A NIGHT AT THE MOULIN ROUGE *(1951)*. *Shot in the Moulin Rouge the-ater in Oakland, California, this girlie film showcases some famous strippers and comedy routines from the days of burlesque.*

MOULIN ROUGE *(1952)*. *José Ferrer plays disfigured artist Henri Toulouse-Lautrec and Zsa-Zsa Gabor appears as famed cancan danseuse Jane Avril in this biopic directed by John Huston. Nominated for seven Oscars, it won for costume design and art direction.*

FRENCH CANCAN *(1954)*. *Edith Piaf makes a rare cameo appearance in famed director Jean Renoir's fictional—Technicolor—tale of how the Moulin Rouge came to be.*

GIRLS OF THE MOULIN ROUGE *(1986)*. *Dancers from the Moulin Rouge strut their stuff in this 60-minute film.*

MOULIN ROUGE! *(2001)*. *A bohemian poet (Ewan McGregor) falls for a beautiful courtesan (Nicole Kidman) in Baz Lurmann's hyper and spectacular musical valentine to Moulin-Rouge-era Paris.*

Complainte de la Butte

BY JEAN RENOIR

La lune trop blême (the moon, too white)
pose un diadème (puts a tiara)
sur tes cheveux roux. (on your red hair)
La lune trop rousse (the moon, too red)
de gloire éclabousse (with glory splashes)
ton jupon plein d'trous (your ragged underskirt)
La lune trop pâle (the moon, too pale)
caresse l'opale (caresses the opal)
de tes yeux blasés (of your indifferent eyes)
Princesse de la rue (princess of the streets)
soit la bienvenue (be welcome)
dans mon cœur blessé (in my wounded heart)

COMPLAINTE DE LA BUTTE

Les escaliers de La Butte (The stairways up to La Butte)
sont durs aux miséreux (are tough on the poor)
Les ailes du Moulin (the wings of the windmill)
protégent les amoureux (shelter those who love)

Ma p'tite mandigote (my little beggar)
je sens ta menotte (I feel your hand)
qui cherche ma main (searching for mine)
Je sens ta poitrine (I feel your chest)
et ta taille fine (and your slim waist)
j'oublie mon chagrin. (I forget my sorrow)

COMPLAINTE DE LA BUTTE

Je sens sur tes lèvres (I smell on your lips)
une odeur de fièvre (a scent of fever)
de gosse mal nourri (of an underfed kid)
et sous ta caresse (and under your caress)
je sens une ivresse (I feel a drunkeness)
qui m'anéantit. (that kills me)

Et voilà qu'elle trotte, (and there she goes strutting about)
la lune qui flotte, (the floating moon)
la princesse aussi. (along with the princess)
Mon rêve évanoui (my disappearing dream)

263

ARRONDISSEMENT 19ÈME

This is perhaps Paris's most rough and trumpled neighborhood. Born January 1, 1860, during the realignment of the arrondissements, the 19th is a mix of old buildings in disrepair, tower blocks (on the hideous side) from the 1960s and 1970s, and lively commerce, all fueled by the immigrants who have been showing up here for over a century. In 1900 more than 80 percent of the population was working class, and it remains so today.

There are some amazing parks in this arrondissement, like the distinctive Buttes Chaumont—formerly quarries, then a dump—with hills and dales and cliffs and ponds and a roughness and romanticism that matches the neighborhood but is very un-French-garden-like. There are no straight lines of trees, nor cut-and-dried paths, although there are still plenty of restrictions about where you can kick a football or play.

Going even farther in the anti *à la française* garden theme is the Parc de la Villette at the very outskirts of town. This, the largest park in Paris, was formerly the central slaughterhouse grounds. Here designer Bernard Tschum totally threw out any idea of composition or methodical arrangement and went for a kind of anarchy. Kids love it.

There are *folies* (kooky structures), sport and recreation areas, playgrounds, a science and technology museum, a music museum/ concert hall, and la Géode (an IMAX cinema in a big metal ball). Unlike almost every single other green space in Paris, however, this a place to play on the grass.

ARRONDISSEMENT 20ÈME

The last arrondissement is a neighborhood of young families and the dead. Père Lachaise Cemetery—the largest green space in Paris—takes up 108 acres and is filled with those who made Paris what it is.

The 20th also seems to be going back to its roots as a neighborhood of *guinguettes* (taverns or cabarets) and the working class. Until Haussmann came along, this area was a collection of small villages. But as he razed inner-city Paris to make way for the neat and clean Haussmann boulevards and apartment houses, the poor fled, landing in the three villages—Belleville, Ménilmontant, and Charonne—that became the 20th arrondissement.

Today the neighborhood is an up-and-coming mixture of immigrants and artists who are attracted by the gritty reality and cheap rents (as artists are wont to be). Those who find Oberkampf *finis* have moved here to get away from the gentrification of the 11th arrondissement. According to the *New York Times* today's population is "Algerians, Vietnamese and hipsters."

As legend goes, Piaf was born here under a street lamp outside 72 rue de Belleville on a cold night in December 1915, and she epitomizes the spirit of the 20th: Her mother was an Italian chanteuse, her father a street acrobat; she lived alternately with her two grandmothers, Emma Saïd ben Mohammed, an Algerian, and her paternal grandmother, a cook at a brothel. She is, of course, buried at Père Lachaise.

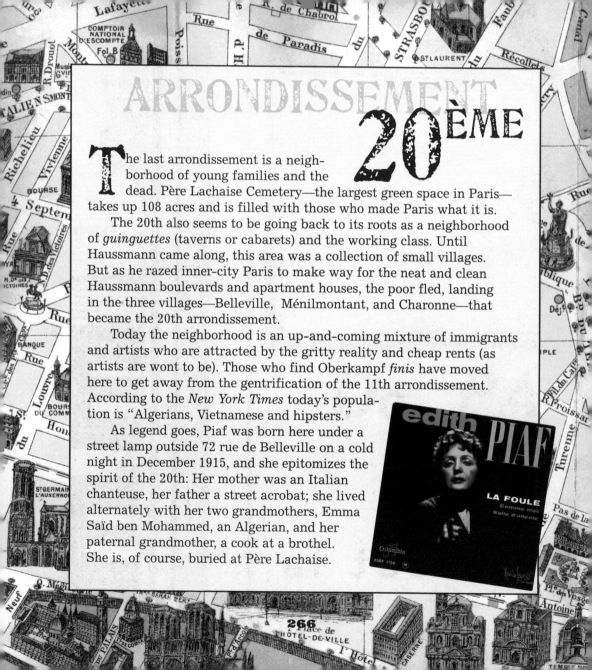

edith PIAF

LA FOULE
Comme moi
Salle d'attente

Columbia

ESBF 1136 (M)

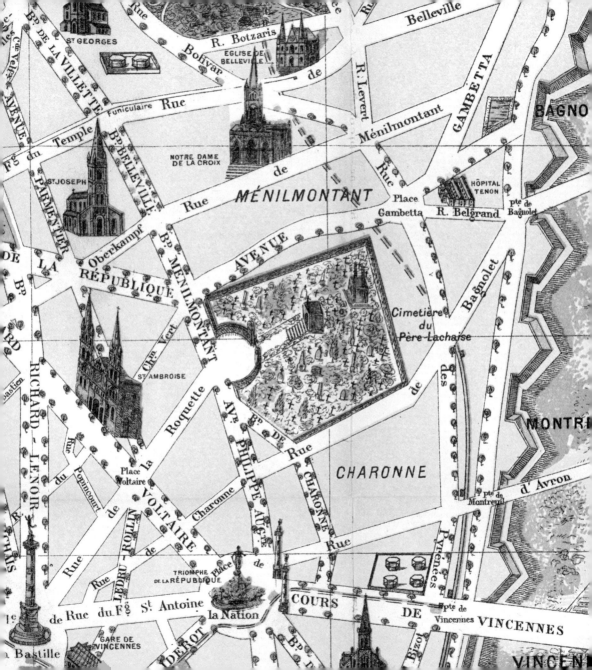

Père Lachaise Cemetery

In the 1780s the rotting corpses buried for centuries in central Paris—especially at le Cimetière des Saints Innocents, directly adjacent to Les Halles, the central food market—finally became too much (the muck, the stench) and prompted the government to ban any further burials within city limits. Twenty years later Père Lachaise—now one of the most visited sites in Paris—opened for business. But because it was so far out of  town back then (in nowheresville), no one wanted to be buried there. A clever marketing campaign that included moving Molière's body and those of two medieval star-crossed lovers (Pierre Abélard and Héloïse), however, helped its popularity. Today the cemetery, containing over 200 years' of fabled Parisians, is the only real museum in the 20th arrondissement—and a beautiful outdoor one at that.

This is a disgusting comedy! This is once again Tout-Paris with its streets, its signs, its industries, its hôtels; but seen through the wrong end of the spyglass, a microscopic Paris, reduced to the small dimensions of shadows, of larvae, of the dead, a human race that has nothing great left but its vanity.

—From the short story "Ferragus" by Balzac, who, along with several of his characters, is buried in Père Lachaise

A final reminder. Wherever you are in Paris at twilight in the early summer, return to the Seine and watch the evening sky close slowly on a last strand of daylight fading quietly, like a sigh.

—Kate Simon, from the guidebook *Paris: Places and Pleasures*

ÉTOILE

LE BOIS DE
BOULOGNE

LES CHAMPS ÉLYSÉ

PALAIS DE CHAILLOT

BORDS

LES